The Professor's Secret

KATIE DEVOE

For CBA

ACKNOWLEDGMENTS

There are so many wonderful people who helped make this book what it is. My editors, Stephanie and Danny, I absolutely couldn't have done this without you. Thanks for keeping me sane. Wendy and Claire, from Bare Naked Words for all of their hard work getting this out. My fantastic friends and family.

i

He stalks towards her, the sound of his footsteps muffled by the plush carpet. She backs away, pulse racing, until she feels cool glass against her back.

There's nowhere for her to go.

He moves in, smiling. "You're trapped."

Desire twists in her gut. "This is a mistake," she says knowing her protest is perfunctory. She's not leaving this hotel room until she's gotten what she came here for.

He undresses, peeling layers of clothing off to proudly display his naked body. Outside, Geneva sparkles in the moonlight, the lake black, still, but here, in this room, nothing matters except the promises of the flesh.

She licks her lips, drinking him in. The broad shoulders. The tightly coiled muscles. His erection, hot and thick against his abdomen.

She glances at the ring on her finger, the diamond sparkling like the lights on the lake below. When she twists it, trying to remove it, he grabs her wrist.

"Leave it." And then he's kissing her with a ferocity she has *never experienced. She melts into him, her body limp, supported by his hand on her waist, his fingers bruising, and the glass behind her.*

He breaks away, panting. "Turn around."

Trembling, she obeys. She stares out at the city. He yanks down her panties and pushes up her skirt. Her nipples ache, the cold glass making them as hard as the diamond on her hand.

Geneva by night. A nameless stranger. A hotel room. She watches the twinkling lights as he whispers in her ear, "Tonight, I own you."

CHAPTER ONE

"Welcome to Intro to Fiction," Natasha Carson says, smiling at the students nervously fidgeting in front of her.

The first day of classes and she's already impatient. Tapping her foot, she scans the room, searching for someone promising, someone to make the semester less tedious. But the usual freshman and sophomores, timid and nervous, do little to excite her.

And then her eyes land on him and she feels an inexplicable tightness in her chest.

She was told a second year grad student wanted to audit her class and she had been too busy to give it much thought. Occasionally, MFA students take undergraduate classes. Now, seeing him sitting in the front row, she feels a buzz of excitement.

Adam LaRue.

Jet-black hair frames his face, just long enough to beg for fingers twining it, tucking it behind his ears. Sculpted cheekbones, a long angular nose, and broad, muscular shoulders.

In the three years she's been teaching at Hudson, Natasha has never seen a more attractive student.

One of those rare men who can be described not just as handsome but as beautiful, without diminishing his obvious masculinity.

His dark eyes follow her across the front of the room, making her aware of her every movement. Something in his expression makes her heart beat just a little faster.

She drops the stack of syllabuses on his desk, trying to ignore the way he's looking at her.

"Take one and pass them along," she says, her voice tight. She turns, smoothing her bright red pencil skirt over her hips, and returns to her place at the front of the room.

They stare at her and she knows they've heard the rumors. That Professor Carson is a cold bitch who likes to fail students just for fun.

It isn't true. She gets no pleasure out of failing people. But she's young and attractive and she knows that if she isn't tough, they'll walk all over her.

"Before we go through the usual introductions, let me be clear. There will be no computers in my classroom. No tablets. No checking Facebook on your phones. In fact, if I see a phone, or hear one ring while we're in class, I will confiscate it. Understood?"

Their eyes widen, this generation who has never lived without cell phones or constant access to the internet and Natasha is once more amazed by the difference a decade can make.

"Now that that's settled, why don't we begin with a brief writing exercise. Hopefully all of you brought actual paper, because for the next ten minutes, I want you to free write. That means, just write. Whatever pops into your head. Forget about punctuation and storytelling. All you have to do is keep your pen moving for the next ten minutes." She unfastens her watch, placing it on the desk where she can see it. "Begin."

She perches at the edge of the desk, legs crossed, expression neutral and studies them. Their baby faces. Their nervous expressions and sideways glances as they write frantically.

Her eyes are drawn back to Adam LaRue. Even with his head down and his hair falling in front of his eyes, he's gorgeous. Black text curls around his bicep, and she has the sudden urge to push up his sleeve to read what the tattoo says.

Her eyebrows knit together. What the hell is she going to do with *that* in her classroom all semester? That gorgeous temptation sitting right in front of her. There should really be some sort of rule against this sort of thing. Students too attractive must be quarantined.

Plus, there's Christopher.

With a wistful sigh, she glances at her watch, surprised to see the ten minutes are already up. "Pens down."

As the rest of the class scramble to finish writing, Adam LaRue just leans back calmly, a ghost of a smile crossing his face as his eyes meet hers.

Natasha inhales sharply. There's something about him that she can't put her finger on. His eyes follow her as she crosses in front of her desk, the way a predator watches its prey, making her hyperaware of the way her skirt pulls across her hips and ass, accentuating her curves.

Her eyes narrow on his handsome face, refusing to let his staring intimidate her.

"You can start," she says, keeping her voice cold and

emotionless.

Those dark brown eyes lick over her, the heat in his expression disorienting, unsettling – when was the last time someone looked at her that way? – and then he begins, his voice a soft, husky whisper and Natasha has to lean forward to hear him. His words wash over her. Sounds. Textures. Slowly, they begin taking shape, gaining meaning.

"I give myself. Give myself wholly. The pain dissipates. The blood rushes in my ears. I am his. Only his. The strike of a hand is the feeling of love. The kiss of the whip a sign of devotion. I give my body, because it is all that is left to give. I give my body, because it is already his."

Her head snaps up, her lips parting in surprise as Adam coolly sits back, his dark eyes trained on her, his expression unreadable. Astounded, Natasha pushes her glasses up the bridge of her nose.

This can't be happening.

But the look he gives her allays all doubt.

She swallows the hard lump in her throat.

He knows.

CHAPTER TWO

"Pull another stunt like that and I'll fail you on the spot," Natasha hisses the moment the door slams shut and they are alone.

Adam's lips twitch, as if he's fighting back a smile, which only fuels Natasha's anger.

He blinks slowly. "I wouldn't dream of it," he drawls in that husky voice of his.

She keeps her eyes on his, refusing to back down, but the way he looks at her makes her want to run for cover.

Finally, he smiles. "I'm really excited for this semester," he says, eyes gleaming with amusement. Hoisting his heavy book bag onto his shoulder, he turns, heading for the door, and Natasha sags with relief until he pauses, glancing back at her. "I'm a huge fan of your work," he says, "and I'd love to discuss your books with you one of these days."

With one last arrogant grin, he walks out of the room.

The moment she gets home, Natasha throws her bag down and heads straight for the bottle of bourbon on the kitchen counter, hands shaking as she pours herself a drink.

How the hell is this possible?

She knocks the bourbon back, savoring the slow burn as it travels down her throat.

She's done everything possible to make sure this never happens. To make sure no one knows. For years, she's lived a double life – respected professor by day, mysterious erotica writer by night.

The words Adam read, stolen words, are hers, burned into her body, as much a part of her as her skin or her heart. It was the end. The crowning moment. The final declaration of love in her first erotic novel.

It marked the beginning of her career. Since then, she's written fifteen books, dark erotica written and published under the penname Layla Allen so that no one, not even Christopher, would ever find out.

Because people like Natasha Carson don't write hardcore erotica and they don't self-publish. She remembers the sneers amongst her fellow MFA candidates whenever someone mentioned the word "self-published." And she remembers reading an interview with a woman who said she was told, in no uncertain terms, that if she published romance novels under her real name, she could forget about tenure.

So Natasha knows exactly what will happen if the truth comes out. At best, she'd be a joke. At worst, she'd be out of a job. And it wouldn't just be Hudson. The truth would follow her anywhere she went. That's the beauty of the information age, right? There's no hiding.

She's fucked.

If he opens that gorgeous mouth of his, if he tells

anyone...Natasha shudders, sloshing bourbon onto the counter as she shakily refills her glass.

She takes her glass and heads for the bedroom, knowing Christopher won't be home for another hour. She yanks open the top drawer of her dresser and stares down at her vast collection of sex toys, letting the possibilities wash over her. She'll have to deal with Adam LaRue eventually, but tonight, there's nothing she can do.

She tosses a riding crop on the bed. Why the hell did he have to be so good looking? If he were just some pimply-faced kid, his threat would have seemed more manageable. But he isn't. On the best of days, he looked like a force to be reckoned with. That dangerous combination of confident and arrogant. Just the type of man Natasha would fall for if things were different.

Natasha throws a blindfold on the bed as well. When Christopher gets home, he'll know exactly what she wants. She strips down to her garter and stockings and crawls onto the bed, her mind racing.

Her nipples ache and her sensitive breasts feel heavy and tender. She sinks into the pillows, grazing her hands down her flank, a slow sensual dance, a prelude to the act itself. Some people think of masturbation as a means to an end. A way to achieve orgasm. But to Natasha, it's more than that. It's an art. It's foreplay. It's desire.

It's the build-up as much as the release.

When her fingers skirt her pussy, she feels her arousal. She closes her eyes and when she does, she sees the cocky expression on his gorgeous face, the hunger in his eyes as he took in every inch of her.

She can't remember the last time someone looked at her with such raw desire.

Is it the power that turned him on, or something else? The belief that he knows her because he knows what she has written?

She forces her mind back to the sensations of her body. The way the cool air feels against her exposed skin. The way her pulse jumps at the base of her neck. Trembling, she imagines the sharp bite of the riding crop against her flesh. The way each strike silences her mind, erasing all that exists before and after so all that remains is the feverish anticipation of the next strike.

The feel of leather running between her legs, wet with her arousal. The tease. The impatience caused by the blindfold. Soft darkness. The maddening anticipation as her mind scrambles to guess what's to come. A sharp blow or a gentle caress? Fear, uncertainty, desire, all woven together until they become one entity, bigger than her.

She slides her fingers over the tight knot of her clit, moaning gently. And when she lifts them to her lips, tasting herself, her hips roll impatiently. Sex is her religion. Eroticism her one true god. She makes her living with it. Spends her days thinking about little else. And often feels as if she is always on the brink of orgasm.

Greedily, she sucks on her fingers, enjoying the taste of her arousal, before plunging them back into her hot, wet pussy with a loud moan.

Her spine stiffens, her ears prick, and she stills, trying to discern if it's the front door she just heard until heavy footsteps fill the apartment. Christopher. Her heart clenches. Her gorgeous man who wants nothing more than to make her happy. He looks every bit the part of distinguished poetry professor, the scuffed leather briefcase, the ties and oxfords and v-neck sweaters that on anyone else would look stuffy, but on Christopher only emphasizes his virility.

He'll see her things tossed haphazardly on the living room floor and know she's home.

She relaxes, continuing the slow exploration of her body as she waits for Christopher to find her.

He'll pour himself a drink, kick off his shoes, loosen his tie.

She wants him to see her just as she is, spread open, painfully aroused, wants him to find her and punish her. Punish her for thinking about another man. Punish her for pleasuring herself without him.

Her heart pounds. She wants to call out for him, but it's the wait that makes this so sweet. When she finally hears him, she opens her eyes and he's standing there in the doorway, watching her, a glass of wine cradled in one powerful hand.

For a moment, all she can do is stare at him. She runs her tongue over her lower lip.

"I missed you."

"I can see that." His eyes roam her body, admiring her with an expression that takes her breath away.

He still looks at her like she is an exotic flower or an angel. Not quite real.

Like he can't quite believe she's his.

His lips pull down when he notices the riding crop at the foot of the bed, making her chest tighten in response. What if he doesn't want to play? What if one of these days, he looks at the crop with disgust before walking out of the room?

She swallows her fear and waits.

With the carefulness he gives to everything, he sets

aside his drink and loosens his tie.

After four years, she still loves his body with the same intensity she felt that first time they were together. Heavy muscles, thick chest hair flecked with grey. His strength and power.

He has a man's body. Confident and sure. Not the slightest bit diminished by his age.

When he pushes down his boxers, she licks her lips, her eyes riveted on his growing erection. Seeing it makes her want to devour him whole.

He comes for her, pressing his lips to hers, kissing her with a hunger matched only by her own. The feel of his cock grinding into her hip. The taste of wine on his lips.

Moaning, she loses herself in the kiss.

He pulls back suddenly, flipping her onto her stomach and knocking the air from her lungs.

"Is this what you want?" he whispers, yanking her onto her hands and knees as she nods frantically.

"Yes, please." Her voice, thick with arousal, catches in her throat.

He kneads her flesh, his large hands engulfing her ass as she grips the duvet tight in her fists, anticipation blinding her.

She doesn't just want this.

She needs it.

The crop hisses through the air seconds before landing hard on her skin, burning her, marking her, the second electrifying, and she yelps, her pussy contracting. She is never as wet as after a good spanking. No matter how hesitant Christopher was initially, he knows what she needs. Knows exactly how to please her. He may not initiate these sessions, more than happy to fuck her without toys or games, but when she puts everything together, he follows the script she's written beautifully.

The second strike makes her flinch and bite her lip.

"Who said you could masturbate?" He presses into her, crushing her under his weight.

"I'm sorry. Don't punish me." The words tumble out of her.

"It isn't punishment if you like it," he growls and she feels that flutter of excitement, that desire for the unknown.

But there is nothing unknown. Nothing new. He hits her again and again. Hits her until her skin burns, hot, pulsing, glorious. Every strike of the crop makes her swollen pussy even wetter.

He hits her until she is reduced to a body, writhing on the bed, panting and begging for more and then, only then, does he press his cock into her.

He enters her with one brutal thrust that forces her forward.

"Oh fuck," she moans, rolling her hips, matching his thrusts. "That's it. Use me!"

He groans in response, fucking her faster, harder, fingers digging into her hips as he pounds into her and she can feel her pleasure building, spiraling, higher and higher, the tightness in her belly.

"Natasha," he moans. "Fuck!" Christopher comes hard, cock pulsing inside of her, his seed filling her as he continues pummeling her, driving her closer to the edge.

Natasha comes with a shout, her body spasming, hips rolling, and they collapse, breathless, in a sweaty heap. Christopher rolls over, pulling her onto his chest and throwing one leg over her body, anchoring her to him.

"I love you," he whispers, fingers splayed protectively across her belly.

She presses her lips to his chest, breathing in their mingled scent. "Me too."

For a moment, she forgets her day. Here, pressed against Christopher, she is home. Here, nothing bad can happen.

But even Christopher's comforting presence can't keep the worry at bay for long. As much as she wants to, she can't stay here. Can't remain in stasis while her mind races, playing out all the possible outcomes. The what ifs. The worst case scenarios. If she remains here, she'll slowly go insane.

With a quick kiss to Christopher's chest, Natasha untangles herself and slips from the bed.

He sits up, scratching his chin, and she can see the hurt in his eyes when he asks where she's going. He wants her to stay. To bask in this post-coital bliss with him. But she can't. She can't lay next to him, pondering all the things she's failed to tell him. The lies of omission. All the times she let him fill in the gaps. Let him paint his own picture.

"I have to get back to work." It isn't a lie. Not really.

"Can't you just forget the book for one night? I bought salmon, I thought I'd make dinner and we could watch a movie."

His frustration makes it easier to leave. She's already pulling on pants, not even bothering with underwear, and she can feel his cum, slick and wet, on her inner thighs.

"I'm sorry. I really have to go. You know, publish or perish." She shrugs, knowing there's nothing he can say to that. He knows the pressure she's under.

"What time will you be back?"

"I don't know. Late. Don't wait up."

Outside, she hails a cab and heads uptown, wondering as she fiddles with her glasses if the cab driver can smell the sex on her. And if he likes it.

CHAPTER THREE

The building is just another run down apartment building on a block that has seen better days. The sidewalks cracked and littered with broken bottles and cigarette butts and when Natasha unlocks the front door, the sharp scent of industrial strength cleaner hits her, almost masking the scent of cat urine.

She could easily afford something nicer, flashier, in a better part of town. But this is what she wants. 500 square feet of freedom. Apartment 5C, a studio with a view of the interior courtyard, which isn't really a courtyard so much as a space used to house garbage cans and broken microwaves and the occasional discarded mattress.

Natasha knows some of her neighbors by sight, enough to exchange nods in the hallways, but no one speaks to her. The name on the mailbox reads Layla Allen. She comes here to write, to get away and it's another secret kept from everyone.

There's no internet. Spotty cell service. All she has to do is turn off her phone and she is truly, spectacularly, alone.

A writer friend once said that in the good old days, before the internet and cell phones, you'd go to a writing retreat and if you didn't feel like writing, you had two options. You could read. Or you could masturbate.

Now, it's all cat videos and emails and constant distraction.

Her studio is a nod to that earlier time.

She pulls a record off the shelf, a Schubert quintet in C Major, and as the music fills the small, cluttered room, she sits down at her desk.

Here, she's Layla Allen. Goddess of smut. Here, she's free.

When she wrote her first novella, *Forced Seduction,* she never expected it to turn into a career. It was just a way to blow off steam during grad school. After two years of workshops, of baring her soul to relative strangers around university tables, writing smut was a relief. Above her computer, she wrote the words: Once upon a time there was a very pretty girl. She was raped. The boy begged for forgiveness and they lived happily ever after.

Those words were her inspiration and she wrote and wrote, words pouring out of her.

Yes. There was a very pretty girl. And yes, she certainly was taken against her will. But she liked it. Loved it, even. Loved the struggle. Loved the pain. Loved fighting to be free. Loved the feeling of a man, stronger than her, holding her down with only the weight of his body, his knee pressing into her thigh, spreading her open as she fought, as she writhed in pain, screamed, all to no avail.

The pretty little virgin didn't stand a chance.

Only the boy didn't beg for forgiveness. He watched

the pretty girl respond to him, watched her orgasm again and again, turned on by the pain and the degradation and he knew, knew he'd found the girl he'd been searching for all along.

It was hot, sweltering, one of those classic New York summers, the stink of garbage wafting up from the street, the smell of charcoal grills, and those long summer nights that seemed to go on forever. She lived off wanton soup and egg rolls from the Chinese restaurant downstairs, taking breaks only to sleep.

In less than a month, she finished the book. She still recalls sitting back, grinning, the wild sense of accomplishment bursting out of her.

That high kept her coming back, time and again.

She remembers thinking, for the first time in a very long time, she was truly, spectacularly happy.

It was her secret and she told no one, not even her girlfriend at the time. Later, when she met Christopher, she considered telling him the truth, but she couldn't bring herself to. Here he was, this handsome, well-respected poet who saw in her the promise of greatness. Why ruin that with the truth? That she spent her days writing smut and masturbating and truth be told, she liked that more than she'd ever liked working on serious, literary fiction.

Things happened so fast. She had an agent. And then her thesis from grad school miraculously sold, and there was the pressure to polish it up, the publisher breathing down her neck, and she did it, she forced herself to do it, but every second felt like she was pulling teeth. When Christopher asked her to move in with him, she did. She applied for a teaching job at Hudson, and to her surprise, she got it. All the while, her smut was selling well and she had money. So she thought, hell, what's the harm?

She found the apartment, furnished it with the basics from IKEA. She didn't care about interior design. All she cared about was that it was functional, practical. And hers.

She rarely thinks about the types of people reading her books, but Adam, with his hipster good looks and literary ambitions, certainly doesn't fit the stereotype in her mind. She always imagined middle aged women, women with kids, families, responsibilities slowly wearing them down, women who don't regret their lives, per se, but who have lost the excitement, every day the same, every day monotonous, women who want just a few moments to escape that reality, to slip into a fantasy where the men are always handsome and the sex is always fantastic.

She likes her life, just the way it is. She likes working without the pressure of anyone breathing down her neck. Likes that no one knows about this part of her. And Adam, with that smug look of his, threatens that balance.

With a sigh, she opens a blank Word document and stares at the screen. Every time she finishes a Layla Allen book, she swears she'll write something serious, but then she gets an idea, something delightfully erotic and she can't help it. Whenever her agent, Meredith, calls to remind her that her two-book contract requires her to actually write, and publish, a second book, she feels a stab of guilt. Meredith would murder her if she ever found out, but somehow, the guilt is never enough to propel her back towards literary fiction.

If Adam tells anyone…the thought consumes her, different scenarios playing out in her mind, the power he wields, the control…

As she begins typing, her fingers flying over the keys,

she feels that familiar buzz, that high that only writing smut brings. Words pour out of her, scenes form, hurried sketches she'll later flesh out.

This isn't a feeling she's willing to give up. This excitement. This fear. As much as she'd like to think otherwise, the truth is, her first novella terrified her. She worried it was too dark, too taboo, worried that if anyone found out, it would call into question all her feminist politics, but she wrote it anyway, never expecting to publish it and only later, when she decided to self-publish, to give it a shot, it felt like a big, liberating fuck you to all that was expected of her.

It felt like freedom.

As her fingers fly over the keyboard, she has only one thought: Adam.

She recognizes him instantly. His face etched in her memory. One night. One night after a conference in Geneva, she made a mistake and he was her mistake and now, as he casually takes his seat, she feels her world collapsing.

When he looks at her, she knows he remembers as well as she does. One night. A hotel room. A nameless stranger from a bar. An escape from the doldrums of married life.

A mistake. Until this moment, she thought she'd been able to forget about it. To pretend it was a dream. That it never happened.

His look brings her crashing down to reality. She hopes he can't see the way she trembles behind the podium.

The next hour and a half are the longest of her life. And as she packs up her notes, he lingers behind, waiting. A predator.

He whispers her name and she remembers everything. The shameless way she begged him to fuck her. Begged him to do to her things she would never have let her husband do.

"Do I know you?" she feigns innocence, feigns forgetfulness but they both know she knows.

His eyes land on her wedding ring. She wore it that night. He wouldn't let her take it off, even after they got to the hotel room. He closes the distance between them, stands too close for decorum's sake. *"Does your husband know about Geneva?"* Amusement shines in his dark eyes. *"Does he know how you screamed for me to fuck you harder?"*

Desire is a hot knot in her stomach. *"Please don't do this."*

He grins. *"There are pictures, you know? Of that night. What do you think would happen if he saw them?"*

Natalia shivers. *"What do you want?"*

He laughs. *"What do you think?"*

CHAPTER FOUR

When, after a last minute cancelation, Thomas Crench, the director of the fiction department, asked her to fill in on a panel on the craft of writing fiction, making it clear she wasn't his first, or even second, choice, she wondered, not for the first time, if he only asked because of Christopher.

Still, she said yes. As much as she hates it, these are the things they look at when considering tenure and given she hasn't been publishing nearly as much as she should be, she doesn't have much of a choice.

At least Maggie's here, though she's sitting on the far side of the panel, too far away to talk to.

Natasha taps her foot impatiently, waiting for it to begin, watching as students spill into the room, their laughter infectious as they grab tiny sandwiches and pour themselves glasses of cheap white wine.

Most of them are only here for the free food and booze.

God, she hates these things. Hated them when she was

a student and hates them even more now that she's expected to actively participate in them. What the hell does she know about the craft of writing? What does anyone know? She fiddles with her notes, knowing she won't need them once they begin. They're only there as a security blanket, a reminder that she is prepared.

From the corner of her eye, she catches Thomas Crench ambling over to the microphone, clearing the phlegm from his throat. Quickly, students fill the plastic folding chairs.

"Welcome to the first installment of our Living Writers series. Let me introduce our panel members. Natasha Carson, author of the novel *Hunger*. Margaret Anderson, author of the novels *Speculation, Clouds of Grass* and most recently, *Succulent Dementia*. And of course, the esteemed Perry Green, who's come all the way from Dublin to teach this semester. He's the author of two critically acclaimed novels, *Tommy* and *The Sycophant* as well as the collection of poetry, *A Well-Stabbed Heart*. Ms. Carson will start off tonight's event."

Natasha fights the urge to roll her eyes. Of course Crench would say "the esteemed Perry Green" while barely acknowledging the accomplishments of the two women who are actually faculty members here.

Swallowing her pride, she gives him a tight smile before beginning. "Is it even possible to teach craft? Are some people born with a certain innate talent that others lack? Certainly, teaching writing, one hopes that the answer is no. That craft is something that can be taught and learned..." The words are rehearsed and she falls easily into the rhythm of it and when she sits back, it's Maggie's turn. After they've all delivered their initial remarks,

Crench begins directing questions at each of them, often steamrolling over Natasha's answers and she lets it go, refusing to be baited into snapping at the insufferable man in front of an audience.

Finally, Crench opens it up for questions from the audience. Natasha expects the usual masturbatory questions designed to show off the intelligence of the speaker, designed to highlight their intellectual prowess that always strike her as a waste of time. A hand in the back of the room goes up and when she sees that it belongs to Adam, she tenses.

He looks directly at her, smiling. "How much of your writing would you say is based on personal experience?" His smooth voice carries easily across the room with just a hint of mischief.

How many times has she been asked this before? In workshops and from interviewers when her book came out? But she knows, from the look in his eyes, that Adam isn't asking about *Hunger*.

"We've all heard the expression, write what you know. But writers, I'd like to stress this is particularly true for female writers or writers of color, are often denigrated for staying too close to personal experience. Great male writers speak to the universal, while female writers, writers of color and queer writers write only about their unique experiences, which of course have no bearing on society as a whole."

She doesn't have to look to know Crench's face is drawn in irritation, which fills her with a twisted sense of delight.

"While obviously, this is bullshit, one has to keep that in mind when writing. Everything I've written, I've written from experience. But what experience? Am I the woman eating her husband's heart on the kitchen floor?" Natasha pauses as laughter fills the room. "Of course not. When I say experience, I mean emotional experience. How can you write about love if you've never loved? How can you write about pain if you've never experienced pain? I am not my characters, but my characters are, in some sense, me."

Natasha turns to Crench, signaling that she's finished, and before Adam can voice a follow-up, he's calling on someone else and Natasha sits back, forcing herself to keep her expression neutral and her posture straight despite the feeling of Adam's eyes on her.

By the time Crench thanks the audience for coming, Natasha feels wrung out and exhausted. Maggie comes over and whispers in Natasha's ear, "How much do you want to bet he'll be giving Green a hand job later?"

Natasha laughs. "Green didn't look too thrilled with the idea."

Maggie shrugs. "You never know. Anyway, I need a drink. The Mark?"

When Natasha looks up, she sees Adam standing against the back wall, talking to an attractive blond. Forcing herself to look away, she nods. "Sure, I just have to run to my office real quick."

"Bless your heart. I'll meet you downstairs. I'd rather gouge out my own eyeballs than sit around listening to more disingenuous ass kissing tonight."

Chuckling, Natasha slips away from the table and cuts through the crowd of students, now busy trying to drink as much wine as possible before it's time to go. She keeps her eyes forward, hurrying past them, refusing to give into the temptation to take one final look at Adam.

Suddenly, the idea of sitting in a dark bar with a strong drink has never sounded so good.

Like Natasha, Maggie teaches in the fiction department and they became friends quickly. More than once, she's listened as Maggie complained about the behavior of certain, more senior, members of the faculty making advances and as much as she hates it, Natasha is thankful that because of Christopher she's never had to put up with that.

No one would dare.

Not with Christopher heading the poetry program.

The thought makes her unspeakably sad. It shouldn't take a man to stop other men from making unwanted advances.

She unlocks her office and ducks behind her desk, searching for the bag she left earlier, a late present for Maggie from her recent trip to London to visit her parents.

"I take it you and Crench don't exactly get along."

She jumps, her head smacking hard against the underside of her desk. With a loud curse, she grabs her bag and stands. Adam is leaning against the doorjamb, his arms crossed casually over his chest.

"You scared the fuck out of me."

He laughs. "Sorry about that."

"I'm sure." She shoves the plastic bag into her purse and takes a quick look around her office to make sure she hasn't forgotten anything.

"Do you have a minute?" He doesn't wait for her response, stepping inside and pulling the door closed behind him, and though his posture is relaxed, Natasha tenses nervously.

"There are so many things I want to ask you. Questions

I'm sure you wouldn't want me asking out there." He motions towards the hall. "For instance, is the infamous Layla Allen nearly as kinky as her books? Or is it an act?"

Natasha straightens up. "That's none of your business," she responds coldly, her fists clenched at her sides as she fights the urge to hurl something at his face.

He laughs. "But I need to know."

"No."

Adam doesn't blink and Natasha hesitates, knowing she'll have to push past him if she wants to leave. The idea of being that close to him, of touching him, even inadvertently, makes her chest tight.

A thought flashes through her mind. Adam, closing the distance between them. Adam, overpowering her. He's a head taller and it wouldn't be hard, all it would take is the right amount of pressure, twisting her arm behind her back and she'd be helpless.

"Oh, come on. Please?" he cajoles. "I'm your biggest fan."

"Absolutely not," she says stiffly, trying to mask whatever it is she's feeling. "I have to lock up so if you'd -" She waves her hand dismissively, almost expecting him to remain as he is, blocking the door, but finally, he steps aside, giving her room to open the door.

"I want to hear all your naughty secrets," he whispers, his voice playfully seductive.

Natasha yanks the door shut, making the pictures rattle against the wall, and when she flips around angrily, she fights the tingling sensation running down her spine, her body's response to his suggestive words.

"No."

With that, she storms past him, listening to his laughter

as it floats behind her.

The Mark is the only half-way decent dive within twenty blocks of campus, a small, dingy place with cheap drinks, a pool table and a dart board, making it a local favorite among grad students, but on a Tuesday, it's quiet and they have no problem finding an empty booth.

Dave, an older Irish man with an easy smile and a generous pour, ambles over as soon as they sit down.

"Welcome back," he says, his thick white eyebrows dancing on his forehead. "Summer ain't the same without you beautiful ladies. What are you having? The usual?"

Natasha, still shaken from her run-in with Adam, orders a double.

"So, tell me all about London," Maggie says, leaning back and spreading her arms along the back of the booth.

London. Natasha pales. With everything going on, she's managed to push aside what happened. Maggie laughs at her expression, seeing right through her.

"That good, huh?"

Natasha makes a face and glances over at the bar, hoping Dave will hurry up with their drinks.

"It could have been better."

"I thought your parents love Christopher."

"Oh, they do. My father gets all chummy, boys club whenever he's there. They actually went to The Arts Club and drank whiskey and smoked cigars." Natasha shrugs. "I got you something." She pushes a plastic bag across the table and Maggie lets out a gleeful squeal.

"Oh, you wonderful, wonderful woman," she says, peering at the tins of Fortnum & Mason tea. "If it's fit for the Queen, it's fit for me."

When Dave returns with their drinks, a bourbon on the rocks for Natasha and a draft beer for Maggie, Natasha sips her drink with her eyes closed, hoping the whiskey will calm her nerves. It's the second day of the semester and she already feels like she needs a vacation. Not just from work but from life.

She wants, more than anything, to tell Maggie everything. The trip to London with Christopher. Adam. All about the smut. Everything. But when she opens her mouth, she can't seem to form the words.

How do you tell someone you've been lying to them for years?

Instead, she asks about Maggie's summer.

"Oh, it was just fucking grand. I hate my book, which is fabulous, because it's due to the editor in, I don't know, three days or something equally dreadful. The awful Marco appeared long enough to give me a fucking yeast infection before driving back to wherever the fuck it is that he lives now. Oh, and my landlord upped the rent by about 1000%. So yeah, life is generally marvelous." Maggie raises her glass.

"You aren't moving are you?" Natasha feels a stab of panic. Maggie's apartment, a loft in a once industrial part of East Williamsburg, reminds her of her life before. If Maggie gave it up, it would mark the end of an era and right now, Natasha isn't sure she could handle that.

"Are you fucking joking? My place is amazing. But this does mean that cheap bastard of a landlord had better repaint and fix the leak in my bathroom." Maggie shakes her head. "You can't charge Manhattan rents and expect your tenants to just roll over and accept the same bullshit lack of service. No sir."

"Maybe don't phrase it quite like that."

"What? You don't think my charming bedside manner will do the trick?" She takes a long sip of her beer. "But seriously, my life is falling apart, please tell me you have some gossip. Nothing puts a smile on my face faster than hearing about someone else's woes and misfortunes."

This is why Natasha loves Maggie. She pats her hand affectionately. "Sorry, there's nothing to tell."

"You're the fucking worst!"

She laughs. "I know, but my life is about as boring as they come."

When Dave comes by to check on them, they order a second round. After all, they haven't seen each other since the spring semester ended in May.

At ten-thirty, Natasha stumbles home, drunker than intended, but somehow, whenever she goes out with Maggie, intentions get thrown to the wayside and drinks just seem to materialize out of thin air. Very Gatsby-esque, she thinks, squinting as she tries to fit the key into the lock on the front door.

On the second try, she gets the door open. When she told Christopher she was grabbing a drink with Maggie, he told her he wasn't waiting up. He knows the drill. And he left the hall light on, the way he always does when he goes to sleep before she gets home, something that's been happening with more and more frequency of late.

London. It all changed in London. And now she feels like she's walking on eggshells, afraid that if they're alone, he'll say something.

What happened to their unspoken agreement to never speak of the future?

She changes into pajamas in the bathroom so she won't wake Christopher up by turning on the bedroom light, but when she crawls into bed next to him, he stirs, rolling over and embracing her in that way that makes if difficult to tell if he's awake or not.

"Did you have fun?" he murmurs, his voice thick with sleep.

"I did. Maggie says hello."

He nuzzles her hair. "God, you smell like a brewery." He rolls back onto his side so only their butts are touching.

"I can take a shower if you'd like," she offers as guilt stabs its way through the haze of alcohol.

"Don't be silly. Go to sleep. I love you."

"I love you, too."

CHAPTER FIVE

"I want to die," Natasha grumbles, shutting her eyes against the blinding morning light filling the apartment.

"I thought you might say that," Christopher says with a laugh. "Coffee?"

"Yes, please!" She flips onto her stomach and pulls the covers over her head, blocking out as much light as possible.

What the hell was she thinking having that last drink?

She reaches blindly for her phone on the bedside table, pulling it under the safety of the covers and squints at the screen as she texts Maggie. *I want to die. I hate you.* She hits send before closing her eyes and falling back on the pillows.

Her phone chirps angrily. *It's seven in the morning. What the hell are you doing up?*

She groans. Maybe it's getting older or else sharing a bed with Christopher for so many years, but against her will, she's become a morning person, the type of person incapable of sleeping past seven-thirty in the morning, no matter what. Some days, she considers it a blessing. But on mornings like this, with her head pounding and her mouth as dry as a desert, it's a fucking curse. At least she isn't teaching until two, more than enough time to nurse herself back to health and at least moderate functionality.

God, she's too old for this crap.

When Christopher clears his throat, she peels the covers back, exposing just the top of her face, embarrassed that he can see how much pain she's in. But if she expects censure, all she gets is an indulgent smile and a freshly brewed cup of coffee.

Seeing the coffee in his hand, she sits up. "You are the most marvelous man alive. I love you so much right now it hurts."

"That's your hangover," he says, placing her coffee on the bedside table with a laugh. "You'll feel better when you've showered."

"Liar!"

He kisses her forehead. "I promise."

With another groan, she shuts her eyes.

You are too fucking old to behave like this, Natasha admonishes herself as she waits for her students to arrive. Way too fucking old.

When the door opens, Natasha doesn't have to look to know that it's Adam. There's just something about him that's impossible to ignore. She sips her coffee in silent rage. Can't he just drop her class and leave her in peace?

Hangovers always leave Natasha in a black mood. The world is ending and she's a terrible person, or something like that. She takes roll, not the least bit surprised to find several students have dropped the class since Monday.

She's proud of her reputation, even if it doesn't always reflect positively on her end of semester student evaluations, which, she's always suspected are stacked in the favor of lazy graders and incompetent professors. Why universities put so much stock in reviews left by students more interested in drinking and hooking up than a decent education is one of the great academic mysteries Natasha knows she'll never understand.

"A little housekeeping first." She pushes her glasses up the bridge of her nose. "As you know, each of you will be workshopping three times this semester. That means we will need to begin next week. So, before I have to start assigning, which is zero fun for everyone, do I have any volunteers?"

Adam is the first to raise his hand.

"Anyone else? We'll be doing three people per class, and I'd really prefer not having to randomly pick."

The redhead, Laura, sitting at the back of the room lifts her hand tentatively. Good, Natasha thinks, at least it won't just be the boys.

No one else volunteers.

She sighs heavily. "Someone pick a number."

"Three," Adam's clear voice rings out.

Natasha counts three from the top of the roster then looks up. "Colin Dryfus. You'll be joining the illustrious first week of workshoppers." She smiles benignly at the room, unable to remember which of the students is Colin.

When his hand shoots up, she has her answer.

"I'm sorry, Ms. Carson, but there's no way I can be ready in time."

She stares at him coldly. "What was that?" she asks though she heard him perfectly. *Ms.* Carson.

Nervously, he looks around, clearly hoping someone will tell him what he's done to piss off their professor while Natasha continues staring at him, deriving a certain satisfaction from seeing him squirm.

"Professor Carson?" he tries again.

"And why, exactly, won't you be able to present? Your colleagues seem perfectly capable."

"It's just..." he trails off, his excuse disappearing under the weight of her unamused expression.

Ignoring a twinge of guilt, she says, "If you have a valid reason, see me after class. Otherwise, I expect all of your stories emailed to the class no later than Saturday evening, let's say, 10 pm."

With that, Natasha begins her discussion of the three fundamentals of story writing, watching their eyes glaze over and she knows they're only interested in writing and not in learning about writing.

She gets it.

After all, she was just like them not so long ago.

Adam stops by her desk, grinning, as the rest of the class pours from the room, eager for freedom. "Hair of the dog?" he asks, crossing his arms over his chest and peering down at her.

"Coffee," she grumbles, angry with herself for being so obviously hungover. Not good. Not good at all. "Is there something I can do for you?" she asks when it's clear he's not leaving.

"I thought we could talk. You know, get to know each other better, that sort of thing."

"Office hours are twice a week before class."

"I don't think this conversation would be appropriate

for office hours," he jokes and Natasha just rolls her eyes.

"You keep this up and I'll fail you anyway."

"I'm auditing, remember? You can't fail me."

"Lovely. Since there isn't anything you want to discuss about class, I suggest you make yourself scarce because if I don't get my hands on a cup of coffee, I can't be held responsible for whatever actions I may take."

Adam laughs. "That sounds promising."

She glares at him over the top of her glasses. "I promise you, it isn't."

"Coffee it is, then."

The coffee stand in the lobby sells over-priced, mediocre coffee and stale pastries wrapped in saran wrap, but Natasha doesn't care enough to go off campus to one of the nicer cafes. Caffeine is caffeine. She orders hers black, no room for milk, and then turns to Adam. "What do you want?"

"The same."

As the barista pours their coffees, Adam reaches for his wallet, but she waves him away, dropping a ten on the counter and not bothering to wait for change. Grabbing her coffee, she heads for the revolving doors, Adam trailing close behind.

The cool air feels like a welcomed balm on her face and Natasha breathes it in, thankful for the coming fall and the coffee to warm her hands as she gazes out at the bustling quad.

Adam stands beside her, and though she is acutely aware of his presence, she does her best to ignore him.

As much as she sometimes loathes teaching, there's something about Hudson's campus that almost makes it seem worth it. The ancient oak trees casting their shade across the grounds. The brick buildings. The constant movement of students hurrying from one building to the next.

To Natasha, it feels like home. The smell of the old card catalogues. The musty rooms filled with books. Even the harried expressions on the students' faces. Growing up, her mother often taught abroad and Natasha and her father always joined her, the one constant in all their travels being the university campuses and their students.

"What kind of trouble did you get into last night?" Adam's question jolts her from her thoughts and she responds carelessly.

"Maggie broke me."

"Freckles?" he asks, laughing.

"*Freckles*," she says, giving him a sharp look, "is one of those maddening people who can drink all night and wake up the next morning chipper and ready to go. I am obviously not one of those people." Natasha frowns. "Not that Maggie's particularly chipper to begin with."

"You naughty things." His dark eyes glisten. "Does someone need to be taught a lesson?"

The heat simmering just beneath his taunt makes Natasha stiffen. He's just goading her, trying to get a rise out of her, trying to see how far he can go before she snaps.

She knows better than to give him the satisfaction of a response. Better to ignore him and hope he gets bored.

Judging by the twinkle in his warm brown eyes, he isn't the slightest bit bored yet.

"Is it really that entertaining to torment me?"

"I don't know what you're talking about," he says with all the feigned innocence of a child caught with his hand in the cookie jar.

She squints at him. "I'm glad my misery amuses you."

He laughs. "It wouldn't be the first time someone called me a sadist and meant it."

Despite his joking tone, Natasha has an inkling that for once, he's being completely serious.

"Don't you have somewhere better to be? Isn't there a thesis you need to be writing?"

"Nope."

"Fantastic."

He laughs again. "I wanted to apologize."

Natasha sputters, nearly choking on her coffee. "Excuse me? I don't think I heard you right because it sounded like you said you wanted to apologize."

"About Monday. I didn't mean to embarrass you in class. The words just sort of popped out of my mouth. *Mea culpa.*"

Natasha narrows her eyes. Adam, with his cool grace, doesn't strike her as a man who accidentally does anything.

"I'm not embarrassed," she says slowly, trying to figure out where Adam is going with this.

"Really?"

"Really."

"Why keep it a secret then?"

"I'd rather my parents never find out I spend my days writing about anal sex and nipple clamps and the subtleties of dubious consent," she says carefully. "Plus, I have a sneaking suspicion that my employment may suddenly be terminated if anyone finds out. Can't have a smut peddler shaping young minds and all that." She takes a deep breath, not wanting to let on how important a secret it is to her. "As such, I'd really appreciate your discretion."

"Oh, I can be very discrete," he says with a meaningful look. "Anyway, they're lucky to have you." He turns so she can't see his expression. "You're a brilliant writer. And a more than competent teacher."

Natasha shoves him, hard and he just laughs, rubbing his arm. "Should you really be abusing your students like this? Just think of what the admin would say," he says in mock outrage.

Natasha, fed up and tired, begins walking away, her heels clicking on the stone steps, but he just jogs down the steps, catching up with her easily.

"So, where are we headed?"

"*I'm* going home. I have no idea where you're going."

"Come on, I feel like the two of us have more in common than you realize. That we could be friends if you just give me a chance. I'm really not such a bad guy."

Natasha stops dead in her tracks before spinning around. Her eyes narrow on Adam's face, the handsome lines of his jaw, the way his eyebrows pull together in curiosity.

"I get it. This is fun for you." She jabs her finger at his chest. "But you know what? It's not *fun* for me. If you want to tell someone, by all means. Who gives a shit if it's my career you take down with you. Because, you know, what business does a smut writer have at Hudson? But just because I write porn for a living doesn't give you the right to treat me like shit," she spits the words in his face and Adam straightens up, his face suddenly serious.

"Shit, I'm sorry." He places one hand on her arm and Natasha shrugs him off, ignoring the sincerity in his voice.

They stare at each other, Natasha fuming, Adam's jaw working as he tries to figure out exactly where he went wrong.

"I'm your professor," she says, wincing at the defensive note in her voice.

"I know that."

"Then treat me with the same respect you'd show your other professors." She spins around, leaving him to stare after her as she storms off.

Let him stare.

She has a great ass.

CHAPTER SIX

When Christopher comes home, Natasha is curled up on the sofa in flannel pajamas, surrounded by takeout menus, the television buzzing in the background. Usually, she heads straight to the studio after class, but today, the idea of facing her computer while reliving the conversation with Adam made her want to hurl.

"What do you want to eat? I'm staaaaaarving," she says, unfolding her legs and coming to her feet. She wraps her arms around Christopher's waist and presses her lips to his chest. He lifts her chin with his index finger before kissing her lips.

"Someone looks much happier than when I left this morning."

She rolls her eyes. "I'm in a terrible mood. My students are monsters. I need greasy food in my stomach or else something terrible will happen. Please don't make me eat kale again. I'll die."

She opens her eyes as wide as possible, making Christopher laugh. He gives her a playful pat on the ass.

"Whatever you want," he says before kissing the tip of her nose and walking towards the kitchen, asking over his shoulder if she wants anything to drink.

"Beer, if we have. Otherwise, seltzer."

"You got it."

She returns to her pile of takeout menus, settling on Thai and throwing the rest in a heap on the floor. She grabs her cell phone. "I'm ordering from Panang. You want the regular?"

"Yes. And an extra order of those fried dumpling things."

"Done and done."

It isn't exciting, but it is comfortable. It's home. Sitting on the couch, her legs tucked under her, Christopher by her side reading while she flips channels on the television, searching for something sufficiently mindless to watch. The food will be here any second and they'll eat in front of the tv, watching a movie and that will be their night. And it's enough.

Sure, it isn't exciting, but it's home.

Who needs exciting, anyway? Exciting only gets you in trouble.

"Ohh, yes!" She tosses the remote aside and settles back, pulling her legs up in front of her. Christopher flicks his eyes towards the screen, frowning.

"Haven't you seen every episode of this by now?"

She grins at him. "Hush. *CSI* makes me unspeakably happy."

He mumbles something about it being the worst show on television, which she ignores. Not everything has to be culturally important.

Some things are just fun.

Takeout cartons litter the coffee table and the room smells like sticky sweet chili sauce. Natasha dozes in front of the television, warm, full, content. For the first time all day, she isn't thinking about Adam.

"Nat," Christopher says in a serious voice that makes her open her eyes, "we should talk."

Her heart begins to beat faster as his words sink in. They've managed to avoid discussing anything that happened in London and she's been hoping, albeit naively, that they can continue ignoring it until it seems like it never happened.

"I meant what I said in London," Christopher adds, as if there's any doubt in her mind what it is that needs to be discussed.

Her stomach turns.

"Please, not tonight," she says softly, turning toward him.

His guarded expression makes her worry that he's afraid if he pushes too hard, she'll walk out of the room and never come back.

How did they get to this point? How did it come to this?

"I meant it," he insists.

Natasha, afraid that if she doesn't stop him now, he won't stop, puts her hand on his knee, angling her body across his so she can silence him with a kiss.

"I know," she whispers, kissing him again. He reaches around her, lifting her onto his lap and deepening the kiss until she's moaning against his lips, her hips rocking over his, his erection hard between them.

Sure, sex doesn't solve everything, but it certainly makes things seem better.

He pulls back, fixing her with an intense stare that makes her pulse quicken.

"Say it," he demands, eyes burning into her and she knows exactly what he wants from her.

"I love you."

"Say it again."

"I love you," she sighs and then his lips are on hers again, tasting her, his tongue teasing as he devours her.

She pulls back long enough to yank her shirt over her head and toss it aside and then they are kissing again, clawing at each other as if they haven't done this a million times before, as if there is anything new. Desperation fills the air, fueling their desire, their need. When he takes her nipple between his teeth, she purrs, impatiently reaching between them, grasping his erection and stroking it forcefully.

She watches his eyes darken and then she leans over, smashing her breasts to his chest and whispering in his ear, "Do you want to fuck me?"

With a growl, he flips her on her back and yanks down her pajama pants, leaning his face over her wet pussy. For a second, their eyes meet, and it's enough to make Natasha's breath hitch and then he's running his tongue over her, one long, slow lick that leaves her quivering for more. And when he sucks her clit into his mouth, her body tenses.

"Don't stop," she begs, but he's already standing up and stripping out of his clothing, his body at once familiar and exotic and then, without another word, he slides his cock into her and she throws her head back as her body pulses with need.

"Harder," she gasps, all thoughts of earlier eclipsed by their frantic coupling, their bodies slapping together in a wild frenzy. "Fuck me harder!"

She wraps her legs around his waist, pulling him deeper.

His lips go slack as he loses himself in her body, and she can feel the pleasure spiraling deep inside of her, deep within, the familiar sensation of Christopher's cock stretching her, opening her, filling her. She pinches her nipples, arching her back off the sofa to meet each punishing thrust and then he's hitting that spot that makes her toes curl and her lips part in a silent plea.

With a shout, she comes, fast and hard and unstoppable, shuddering, panting, her eyes unfocused, her entire body convulsing around Christopher as he continues fucking her, continues pounding into her, marking her as his.

She watches him through half-closed eyes, his head thrown back, this blond giant of a man who looks, in this moment, like a proud lion.

When he comes, she feels him filling her with his hot release and then he collapses onto her, his body hot and sweaty and she wraps her arms around him, kissing his neck.

For the first time in a long while, Natasha doesn't dash out of bed first thing in the morning. Her book can wait. Instead, she stretches out beneath the covers, smiling, content, sated.

From the other room, she hears the shower running, Christopher washing away the reminders of last night and his morning run in the park.

She sits up and waits for him to come back to bed, knowing, as the blankets pool around her naked body, that she will have no trouble convincing him to put off whatever it is he has planned for the morning.

The look he gives her when he finds her still in bed, with no intention of getting up, fills her with sadness, which she hides beneath a cocky grin.

"Come back to bed," she coos as he stands in the doorway to the bathroom, toweling himself dry.

When he drops the towel to his feet, kicking it aside, she feels a flutter in her chest.

"Gladly."

She giggles as he launches himself at her, burying his face in her neck, kissing her excitedly.

They spend the weekend at home. Natasha doesn't go to her studio, and though she feels that needling sensation that there's something she should be doing, she ignores it to spend the weekend with Christopher, reading, relaxing, letting him take care of her. She prepares for her classes. She tries to live in the moment, to enjoy what she has, their familiar routine, their ease together, and to forget about Adam completely.

She's reminded of those early weekends when she first got together with Christopher. When she was twenty-six and the idea of bagels and coffee and lazy Saturday afternoons in bed with *The Times* was exotic and new.

But Saturday night, when she checks her email, she is yanked back to reality. Adam has already sent out his first story for workshop and there it is, sitting in her inbox, a silent taunt. She prints it out, dreading reading it, but knowing that she can't ignore it, and so she gets into her pajamas and sits in bed, propped up with pillows, a pen in one hand, a legal pad beside her and begins reading.

When she finishes, she lets out a ragged breath, struck by a sudden wave of guilt. She expected something graphic and sexual, written with the sole purpose of getting a rise out of her, some twisted perversion of all she's written as Layla Allen. Instead, *this*. She isn't surprised by his lyricism, the lush details and tactile prose. These are qualities she expects from a poet. No, what surprises her is that his story, for all its faults, moves her. The nightmarish landscape. Broken bodies and broken souls. And underneath that, a desperation, a hope, that's nearly crushing in its optimism.

She sits in bed, the manuscript unmarked, trembling, shocked by her sudden desire to reach out and hug him.

When Christopher comes in, she grabs her glasses off the bed, putting them on so she can see him.

"Do you know Adam LaRue? He's a second year," she asks cautiously.

He pauses, one hand on his belt buckle. "Yeah, he's taking my poetry workshop this semester. Why?"

"What's your impression of him?"

Christopher doesn't rush to answer, a quality Natasha has always admired. The way he never jumps to rash proclamations. Every word he says is carefully thought out before it enters the world.

"He's talented and he has a unique voice, but sometimes he seems distracted. Like he hasn't quite figured out what his focus is." He shrugs, pulling the belt from his pant loops and for a moment, Natasha forgets Adam as she stares at the belt in Christopher's hands and all the possibilities it brings, sensual and painful and perfect.

When he tosses it aside to unbutton his pants, the moment disappears and Natasha looks down at the story she holds between her hands.

It isn't complete. It isn't perfect. But perfection is overrated. Perfection is cold and emotionless and inhuman. She frowns, battling the urge to break the cardinal rule of workshop and ask, How much of this is true?

CHAPTER SEVEN

After reading Adam's story, Natasha is anxious to see him again. Whatever happened the last time they spoke isn't forgotten, but she can put it aside, her thoughts now focused on the quality of his writing. She knows her attraction to him is dangerous and that it's made more dangerous by what he's written, because there are few things that leave Natasha as sexually stimulated as the perfect pairing of talent and intelligence, but as she waits for her students to show up, she tells herself that whatever interest she has in him is purely academic.

She has no desire to hurt Christopher or blur the boundaries between professor and student. Those boundaries, which once seemed so trivial to her, are now sacrosanct.

God, her college friends would piss themselves laughing if they could see her now. Natasha, who never believed in boundaries or the forbidden, suddenly tied to them, not just respecting them, but touting their necessity.

What the hell happened?

She grew up. Now, actions have real and measurable consequences whereas before, when she was younger, consequences could be ignored or laughed off, dismissed with little more than a flip of her wrist.

"Okay, let's get to it," she says once the class has assembled. "Remember, we're here to help each story develop into the best story it can be. Which means," she pauses meaningfully, "criticism should be constructive, otherwise keep it to yourself." She looks at the fifteen faces in front of her and wonders who is the most likely to cry, the one to crack under the pressure of workshop, but she doesn't know them well enough to answer. But she's been in enough workshops over the years to know that crying isn't that unusual, though it always makes her uncomfortable.

Natasha Carson has never cried in a workshop, but then, Natasha Carson doesn't believe in public shows of emotion.

Stiff upper lip and all that.

She hopes that this bunch will be heartier than the last group, because nothing ruins her day like trying to quell a student's tears in the middle of class. This isn't pre-school. She shouldn't have to hold their hands and tell them the world is a kind, understanding place.

She looks quickly at Adam, unable to resist and he is watching her with the same calm curiosity as always. He doesn't look the slightest bit nervous but then, this isn't his first time at the rodeo. He's spent a year having his work ripped to pieces by graduate students. And though she doesn't know poetry students well, if they are anything like the fiction students her year, they're a ruthless bunch who enjoy nothing more than watching the weakest one go down.

She'll leave him for last.

"Laura," she says, smiling at the redhead who is once again hiding in the back row, "will you please read the first three paragraphs of your story?"

The first workshop goes surprisingly well. Everyone is respectful, no one cries, and their comments, while not always brilliant, are at least thoughtful, showing they not only read the stories but took the necessary time to think them over.

She expects Adam to linger after class, but he's the first out of his seat. She knows that she should be relieved. That whatever she feels for Adam LaRue, whatever mix of frustration and sexual attraction, it's better if he keeps his distance.

So why, when he darts out the door without so much as a backward glance in her direction, does it leave her feeling like something has been left unfinished?

As the 1 train hurdles uptown, the chill of the subway car making the hairs on her arms stand up, Natasha tells herself it's nothing more than the nervous tension she always feels after taking a few days off from writing. Ask any writer and they'll tell you, writing's a drug.

And Natasha, like most writers, needs it to stay sane.

She needs to get the thoughts out on paper, so she can go home at the end of the day feeling free.

Since she began writing smut, she's taken few breaks, telling herself that it's a competitive industry and she needs to keep publishing or she'll be forgotten. But she knows that's not really it. Her books do fine. But she keeps writing like an insane person, churning out books at a speed that would astonish most writers, because if she doesn't, if she stops, even for a few days, she'll be forced to think about her life and that's something she isn't prepared to do.

So she tells herself she's like a shark, swimming to stay alive.

Except as it turns out, sharks don't need to keep moving to breathe. That's just a myth.

Once inside, she tugs open the windows of her studio, letting the fresh city air clean out the unused smell of her studio. And then she opens the document on her computer labeled *Blackmailed.*

She's playing a dangerous game, but she can't stop. The set-up is irresistible. The gorgeous, dangerous student blackmailing the attractive professor, threatening to expose her secret if she doesn't do as he demands. Of course, her secret isn't that she writes erotica. Her secret is that once, two years before, she went out and had a few too many drinks and a one-night stand with none other than the man now taking her graduate seminar.

It wouldn't matter, of course, except that the professor in the story is married.

And now that the student has had a taste of her, he wants more. He wants everything.

It's exactly the type of story her readers love. The blurred line between consent and desire. The emotional blackmail. The submission.

She tells herself that whatever similarities it may have with her real life, it's ultimately just fiction.

Wind lashes the trees. Wet, dripping branches slap against the windows. Outside, nothing but stormy darkness. Inside, warmth.

The office is empty. Everyone left early. Because of the storm. Because of whatever. And so, she finds herself alone in her office, waiting it out. Hoping that it will eventually end. It has to end. She's wearing $800 pumps. There is no way she's walking anywhere right now.

She doesn't hear the knock on her door. If there is even a knock. She faces the window, watching the storm howl and rage. It's beautiful. Untamed. A reminder that nature is not kind, but destructive.

When he touches her hip, she jumps but doesn't turn around.

"Did you really think you could get away from me that easily?"

His voice is sharp, like a knife against her skin and she shivers, refusing to turn. Because one look into his eyes and she's done.

He'll see the desire painted across her face.

He'll know.

"I own you," he whispers. "I've owned you since Geneva. Turn around."

She obeys without hesitation, keeping her eyes locked on the floor in front of her.

"Look at me."

She looks up. His eyes are as wild as the storm raging outside and his lips curve into that wicked half-smile that makes her panties wet and her nipples hard.

"On your knees."

CHAPTER EIGHT

The shrill ringing of her phone jars Natasha out of the scene and back to the real world. When she sees Christopher's name blinking on the screen, it feels like a silent accusation.

"Where are you? The Poetry Fellows will be here in an hour."

"Fuck!" A quick glance at the clock tells her it's almost six and she's completely forgotten about the Fellows coming over. "I'll be home in half an hour. Need me to grab anything?"

"Another thing of brie?"

"No problem."

An hour later, when the doorbell rings, Natasha is wearing a black and white shift dress and her favorite heels. Every semester, Christopher invites the six poetry fellows over to the apartment for drinks. The fellowship, which includes a substantial financial award as well as a job in the office, confers a certain prestige on the chosen second year students. It isn't a position they apply for; instead, they're nominated by their professors and then selected by a committee based on pieces submitted to workshop the previous year. It's just another way the writing program keeps the students on their toes, constantly looking at each other as the competition rather than fellows in arms.

Christopher, as the director of the poetry program, oversees them. He calls each one personally to inform them of the decision and he meets with them regularly during their second year, acting as a mentor and often friend.

She knows how important it is to him, how much he loves having them over, giving them a peek into his life, their life, but Natasha hates it, hates the way they look at her, the way the treat her, but there's nothing she can do but smile and pretend it doesn't bother her.

Her smile freezes on her face when she opens the door to find Adam standing in the hallway outside their apartment. He's wearing black jeans, scuffed Converse, and a leather jacket over a white t-shirt and the effect is part bad boy, part brooding intellectual.

"Of course," Natasha says, gritting her teeth and turning to head back into the apartment. Of course he's one of Christopher's Poetry Fellows. Of course he's showing up, unannounced at her home.

"Wait."

She hesitates, Adam's husky voice leaving her momentarily speechless and as she stands there, frozen, he leans down, lips brushing her ear and whispers, "Do you have any idea how many times I've fantasized about being inside of Layla Allen's apartment?" She catches a whiff of his cologne mixed with cigarette smoke and leather and when he pulls away, she bites back a sigh. "I always imagined a much warmer welcome."

He steps back, grinning wickedly as his eyes trail brazenly over her body, causing a blush to spread across her chest.

"You look ravishing."

Ravishing. With a word, the spell is broken and Natasha spins around, heading straight for the bar. The fact that he's here, in her apartment, their apartment, and hitting on her with no remorse makes her hands shake with rage.

The fact that his words have any affect on her turns that rage to unease.

Sinking into her favorite armchair, she gulps her wine, listening carefully as Christopher and Adam exchange greetings in the hall, listening for anything more than just casual remarks, and then Adam strolls into the living room like he owns it, taking it all in, every last detail of her life and Natasha, watching him, feels suddenly exposed and vulnerable.

"It's a lovely apartment," he says, taking a seat on the couch.

"It's Christopher's," she responds defensively.

"I figured as much."

The vein at her temple pulses. He has no right. No right to come in here and judge her.

"Given everything I know about you, I expected a St. Andrews Cross and portraits of naked women." He motions to the abstract art adorning the walls. "Or floggers. Floggers would make fantastic wall décor, don't you think?"

"You don't know anything about me."

"Really?" One eyebrow quirks up. "I know you like keeping secrets. That you have everyone fooled with this act except me. I know that under all this, there's a wild woman dying to get out."

She glares at him, refusing to admit, even to herself, that there might be some truth to his assessment, that it might be possible that this man knows her better than the one standing in the kitchen, the one who promises to love her until forever.

Instead, she leans forward, keeping her voice low. "I need you to stop."

Something in her voice makes him look up in surprise, realization dawning on him. "He doesn't know?"

She nods, feeling like this is a betrayal of the worst kind. "I'd really like to keep it that way," she says tightly.

"What are you afraid of?"

"Nothing."

He lifts one eyebrow. "Really? That's not what it looks like to me. It looks like you're petrified he'll find out the truth about who and what you really are and he won't be able to look you in the eye." Natasha stares at him, her heart pounding in her chest. "But I know you and I'm not looking away." The intensity in Adam's face, the way he studies her, makes Natasha shiver and finally look away.

What are you so afraid of?

Everything, a voice whispers in response.

"Who does a man have to fuck around here to get a drink," Adam jokes, casually dropping the subject, at least for now, and Natasha points to the bottles lined up on the cart by the windows.

He stands slowly, brushing his palms over his thighs.

"Want anything?"

She shakes her head, hating herself for the way her eyes hungrily follow him across the room. Hating herself for finding him so irresistible, when all she wants is to hate him. Hating herself for the way her fingers twitch, dying to reach out and tuck his unruly hair behind his ear.

She forces herself to look away, digging her nails into her palm as she stares at the books on the bookshelf, trying to forget about the man standing so close to her.

"How long have you lived here?" he asks, returning with a glass of whiskey.

"Three years, I think." Like she doesn't remember the exact moment Christopher asked her to move in, the smell of the sea air blowing in her hair, and the exact moment, weeks later, when she finally agreed.

"That's a long time."

"I suppose."

Christopher appears, carrying a heavily laden cheese platter, and when he sees them sitting together, he smiles. "Great, you've met Natasha." He stands behind her, resting one hand on her shoulder, the innocent gesture just a touch possessive and Natasha tenses self-consciously, aware that Adam is studying her, and that nothing, not the slightest twitch or movement, will go unnoticed.

"We actually already know each other." Adam pauses and in that pause, Natasha hears a million possibilities. "I'm taking her Intro to Fiction workshop."

"Oh right, I think you mentioned that. How's it going? I hear she can be quite a ball-buster."

Adam laughs while Natasha bristles, hating that expression. Ball-buster. She reminds herself that the condescension she hears is only in her mind.

"I think it's going pretty well, but that's probably a better question for your wife."

Christopher's hand tenses on her shoulder, just for a second, the word wife hanging in the air between them, and then he lets out a laugh, his hand relaxing. "Oh, we aren't married. Nat doesn't believe in anything as conventional as marriage."

In the strained silence that follows, no one speaks. Natasha stares at her wine glass, knowing she should say something, anything to ease the tension. She doesn't have to look up to know that Adam is staring at her, that this moment confirms everything he thinks he knows about her, about her relationship, about Christopher.

She lifts her glass to her lips and takes a measured sip, already knowing what Christopher will say if he thinks she's drinking too much.

They're our students.

Your students. And you invited them to the house.

A pointless fight. He's right. He's always right.

The doorbell rings, making Natasha jump, but even as she's trying to ease out of her seat to answer it, to get away, Christopher's hand presses her down. "I'll get it."

He walks off, leaving her alone with Adam.

"Trouble in paradise?"

Natasha shoots him a look that would make most people cower, but Adam doesn't so much as blink. He leans forward until their faces are only a few inches apart and she can feel the warmth of his breath on her cheeks. "Who wants to be conventional when you can be extraordinary?"

"What the hell do you want?"

The smile Adam gives her, slow and seductive, makes

her nipples tighten beneath the silk of her dress.

Why the hell does he have to be so damn good looking?

Why the hell does her body have to respond to him?

"What do I want?" he drawls, rolling the words around his mouth like a fine wine. "I want to know all your secrets. What makes you tick. What gets you off. What you think about when you're alone. What you dream about when you touch yourself." He voice is calm, his expression neutral, but Natasha feels the heat of his words on her skin.

Natasha says nothing because there is nothing for her to say.

When Christopher returns with the next fellow, Natasha relaxes somewhat, hoping that at least when they are not alone, Adam won't be able to keep pressing her.

There are six fellows in total and while they're all introduced to Natasha, she forgets their names as soon as they are said aloud. She should get up, mingle, make them feel welcome, after all, that's what Christopher expects, that's her job for the evening. Dutiful host. Gracious partner. But she can't. Not with Adam judging her every move, her every word, dissecting her life.

She nurses her drink, silently stewing. Why does he insist on inviting them to the house? He knows it makes her uncomfortable, she's told him that a million times, that they don't look at her the same way, that they treat her like a bug under a microscope. That they've all read *Slaughter-Dew* and they all know that he wrote it about her. But he never hears her. He tells her she's just being silly, that they hold her with the same esteem they hold him with.

She wants to laugh.

This is the price you pay for working together. The price you pay for dating a man fifteen years senior. Motives are questioned. They think you're nothing more than a pretty face.

She doesn't even realize her glass is empty until Adam offers to refill it. She looks at him in surprise, amazed that he's still sitting on the couch instead of off with the rest of them.

"Sure."

Silently, she's thankful for the attention, for not making her feel invisible in her own home.

Christopher's home, she reminds herself. This is Christopher's home. She's merely a guest. A visitor.

She shifts her gaze back to Adam, uncrossing and recrossing her legs as she watches him, realizing that she knows nothing about him. Nothing except that he is a poet and a reader of smut and a troublemaker. Otherwise, he's a mystery.

He's taken off his leather jacket and the tattoos that first attracted her attention are visible now.

"What's it say?" she asks, pointing to the script on his inner bicep. He looks down at it, frowning.

"Oh, you know, the sort of thing stupid boys get tattooed on their arms when they think they're in love."

"You'll have to be a little more specific. I'm not sure I know the preferences of stupid boys in love."

He laughs, leaning back and crossing his ankles. "Catullus."

Smiling, all she can say is, "God, you were that kid, weren't you?"

"Which kid?"

"The one with the beat up copy of *Paris Spleen* shoved

in your back pocket, looking just so terrible deep."

"Nailed it." His easy smile shows no remorse or embarrassment for the adolescent he once was. "I moved around a lot. Books are a natural companion for a kid who doesn't know where he'll be going to school in six months."

"Army brat?" She has a hard time imagining Adam growing up on Army bases.

"No, dad worked for a big hotel chain. I was born in London, but we lived in Paris, Madrid, Berlin. Stockholm for a brief period."

"You have an American accent."

"Bounced from one American school to the next." He sips his whiskey. "I only moved to the States for college."

"That must have been exciting," she says, knowing how flat the words sound and Adam just lifts one shoulder casually.

"I guess. You don't make a lot of friends that way, though."

"Tell me about it."

Adam lifts one eyebrow in surprise.

"Mom's a professor and dad's a journalist. We spent a lot of time in Europe. At least I always had New York to come back to."

"They left?"

She nods. "A few years ago. They're in London now."

For a moment, Adam's eyes lose focus. "Do you ever wish you had a home to go back to?"

She looks away, wanting to give him the privacy to recall whatever it is that makes him look so sad. Across the room, she sees Christopher, standing like a king surrounded by his adoring court. How many times has she secretly resented him his childhood home, practically unchanged since he moved away?

All around them, voices rise and fall, the steady buzz of conversation but she hears nothing. Christopher uncorks a bottle of wine one-handed, and when their eyes meet, he grins. There are moments, moments like this, when he reminds her of a child, capable of the most authentic, earnest joy.

"I'll be right back." She pushes out of her seat, hurrying from the room, stopping only to squeeze Christopher's arm as she passes. She locks herself in the master bathroom and stares at her reflection in the mirror. She's pale. The dark circles under her eyes barely hidden by her glasses. She can do this. Just a few hours and then they will leave and she'll get into bed and everything will be fine.

Everything is fine, she thinks, splashing cold water on her face, letting it drip off her nose, her chin, little splashes on the vanity.

I know you and I'm not looking away.

Natasha shivers. Is everything really fine?

When she steps back into the hallway, laughter and voices hit her hard in the chest, making Natasha want to run back into the bedroom and bar the door until everyone has left. Except eventually, Christopher would come looking for her. He'd worry. Or else, he'd tell her to stop being so selfish, it's just one night.

When Adam steps into the hallway, she feels her face freeze into a rigid mask. He walks towards her, his movements graceful, his eyes drawn. Natasha's heart races. And when he finally stops, he's standing right in front of her and she has to angle her head back to look at him, even in heels.

"What do you want, Adam?" she asks again, her voice catching. The hallway acts as a barrier. The sounds of the people in the living room seem suddenly far away.

"You know what I want." His voice is husky and low. She steps back, desperate to regain her footing. He looks at her with such hunger, such desire, it makes it hard to breathe.

"Adam…" she says, shaking her head.

His eyes darken and he closes the space between them, the heat of his body radiating off him, his proximity maddening. "What do I want?" he repeats her question like the answer is glaringly obvious. "I want you. I want to lick every inch of your body. I want to see the look in your eyes when I make you come. I want to taste you. Fuck you. Sate you. I want everything. And then I want more."

"I'm practically married."

"And?"

"It's never going to happen."

"We both want this."

"Don't…"

"We're adults. We can be discrete."

"Stop it."

He shakes his head. "I want you. I've wanted you from the moment I read *Forced Seduction*. When I read Christopher's book, I needed to know the woman who inspired it. You aren't simple. You aren't civilized. This," he waves his hand in front of him, "this is artifice. This is bullshit. The real Natasha Carson is wild. She's insatiable. She would never allow herself to be caged. Not by a man. Not by an apartment. Not by anything as trivial as material possessions."

This can't be happening. Natasha feels her throat closing up, her tongue heavy as she struggles to speak. "Adam, you have to stop."

She glances frantically towards the living room, but everyone is too busy fawning over Christopher to notice. For once, she's thankful that she's nearly invisible to the poetry fellows.

Adam's eyes burn into her. "I'll wait. You're worth waiting for. But Natasha, I promise you, one day, I will fuck you. I will tie you to my bed and make you scream. And we both know you'll love every second of it. You'll beg me never to untie you."

Reaching over, he brushes the pad of his thumb across her lower lip, making her quiver. And just as quickly, he withdraws his hand, leaving her panting, speechless, staring at this gorgeous man who makes her want to set fire to her life and do things she shouldn't do. Can't do.

Things she wants, desperately, to do.

"Natasha, I think you should look long and hard at yourself in the mirror and ask what the hell it means that you keep something so fundamentally important about yourself from the man you claim to love."

Adam turns and walks away, leaving Natasha to contemplate the truth of his words.

When she finally pulls herself together and returns to the living room, Adam is gone.

CHAPTER NINE

The first time she saw Christopher, he was sitting alone outside the main building at the writing retreat, drinking coffee one morning. He held the mug like it was something precious, something beautiful.

That's when she noticed his hands. Hands you could write books about. Hands you could fall in love with. There was a smudge of ink between his thumb and forefinger and she thought, What I wouldn't do to be allowed to lick those hands clean.

In that moment, she didn't think about Madison, the girlfriend she left behind in New York so she could write in the hills of Vermont for six weeks. She thought only about those hands. Perfect, rugged hands.

At twenty-six, she was the youngest person at the prestigious writing retreat and there were moments when she wondered what the hell she was even doing there. She'd finally turned in her thesis, a first draft of the book she'd eventually publish, and while it was good enough for her to graduate, it wasn't good enough for Natasha. She wanted it to be perfect. She wanted every word to echo with meaning. So she'd applied to writing retreats with the hope that leaving the city would make a difference. That she'd be able to finish the book, really finish it.

And then she saw Christopher and she forgot all about the book. She knew who he was. Christopher Worthington. So she hid her insecurities behind a bright smile and pointed to an empty chair. "Is this seat taken?"

He looked up slowly, surprised, and then smiled. And she was struck by just how blue his eyes were. She'd never seen eyes that blue before.

"Don't be silly, no one wants to sit with me," he joked, placing his coffee cup on the table and extending one hand and she stared at that hand, that beautiful rugged hand and licked her lips before finally placing her hand delicately in his.

Even though his touch was gentle, she could feel the power beneath it.

"Natasha," she whispered and he laughed again.

"My dear, there isn't a person here who doesn't know who you are."

It was harmless flirtation. She knew he was married. The gold band on his ring finger made that clear and he sometimes spoke about his wife, not with passion, but with kindness.

She didn't understand it then. Now, she knows what it's like to be in love with someone, comfortable with someone. Passion fades and what remains is something quieter but no less powerful.

As the weeks passed, she thought less and less of Madison, in New York, waiting for her to come home. All she could think about were those hands, those fingers and all the things they could do to her, if only it were allowed.

Looking at those beautiful, rugged hands, she thought, Here is a man who could skin me a lion.

She never expected him to divorce his wife for her. No, the best she could have hoped for at the time was an affair. Illicit. Passionate. Short lived. She imagined kissing him, the feel of those hands on her arms, the taste of his mouth. At night, after dinner, she'd go back to her cabin and fantasize about fucking him.

But nothing happened. They talked and laughed and went for walks around the retreat, the bright green summer foliage, the smell of dirt and suntan lotion, flies buzzing noisily. She followed him around, in love, if not with the man, at least with the idea of the man. Christopher holding branches out of the way for her, teasing her for being such a city girl, for having the wrong shoes for hiking and never remembering to carry a water bottle.

And he was brilliant, just brilliant. She asked him once, why he became a poet, and he laughed, making the wrinkles more pronounced at the corners of his bright blue eyes and said, I wanted to be a rock star but I couldn't carry a tune. And poetry, it's all rock and roll. And he was serious. Completely, breathtakingly serious.

The attraction wasn't just physical. She wanted to crawl inside his brain, wanted to pick him apart, wanted to learn everything about him.

When it was time for him to leave, he wrote his phone number on the title page of a dime store mystery novel and told her to give him a call some time when she was back in

New York.

She still has the book, sitting on her desk in her studio apartment. On the cover is a woman in red, one strap of her slinky dress slipping off her shoulder, smoking a cigarette. And in the shadows in the background, a man leans against a car, watching her, and it's impossible to know if he's watching out for her or about to attack.

It's the one thing she keeps in the studio to remind her of her real life, the life back home, the life with Christopher.

She got back to New York and it was so hot and sticky, overwhelming after six weeks in the country, the noise, the congestion, and there was Madison, waiting for her outside Penn Station, with an enormous iced coffee from Dunkin' Donuts, wearing cut-offs and a tank top.

Seeing her on that crowded New York street in her dollar store sunglasses, Natasha realized with shocking clarity that it was possible to love more than one person at the same time.

They took the subway back to Madison's railroad apartment in Williamsburg and spent the afternoon making love. Sweaty, hot, sticky love with only a crumpled sheet on the bed, the bright glow of summer filling the apartment. After six weeks imagining Christopher's body, Madison was like a dream, her limbs strong but soft, her muscles supple, her breasts small and firm, her pierced nipples always hard.

She felt like she could have spent a year between Madison's legs without ever getting tired.

They went to the farmers market on Saturdays and walked around the park, stopping to stare at the dogs in the dog park until the stench of urine became too strong and they'd move on, slowly, always in a daze, like they were on drugs, only they weren't on drugs, it was just the effect of the suffocating summer heat.

She often thought about Christopher, in his air-conditioned apartment uptown, his beautiful wife, so prim and proper on the book jacket of her latest novel, with that sly smile of someone who knew which fork to use at a fancy dinner party. She imagined them at literary parties, well dressed, sipping expensive drinks, laughing at the right moments.

That wasn't the Christopher she dreamed of at night, as Madison slept beside her. The one she wanted, the one she'd caught a glimpse of standing barefoot at the edge of a stream, was the Christopher who wrote such wonderful muscular, Anglo-Saxon poetry, all blood and sinew, the Christopher who could gut a fish without blinking an eye.

The Christopher who became a poet because he couldn't be Mick Jagger.

She can't remember why she texted him, only that Madison was in the shower and she stared at his phone number written in that slanting heavy hand of his, so undeniably masculine, for a long time before she worked up the courage.

She felt stupid as she held her breath, waiting for a response. Light-headed. Nervous. But most importantly, excited.

She almost expected never to hear from him again, that he would let her off the hook, but no. He wrote her back immediately, saying he was happy to hear from her and inviting her out for a cup of coffee in Greenwich Village. He knew she lived in Brooklyn; she knew he lived on the Upper West Side. Maybe he wanted to meet somewhere that was equally inconvenient for both of them, but she couldn't help but wonder if his real motive was anonymity.

Her heart raced. She considered putting her phone away, ignoring his invitation until later, but what was the point? She knew she'd be there, waiting for him.

She thought about Madison, rubbing Dr. Bronner's Peppermint soap all over her lithe body, over tattoos and muscles and hairless flesh. She glanced at the open bathroom door before saying yes. And then she stripped naked and got into the shower with Madison, the peppermint scented steam filling her nostrils.

How it burned when it got into the folds of her vagina and how little she cared in that moment.

She pressed Madison against the tiled wall and lapped up the water running between her small, perfect breasts. Madison's soft, breathy moans eclipsed by the running water. Her slick, slippery skin like a dolphin.

And then Madison, grabbing her by the shoulders, turning her around roughly. Madison who kicked her legs open, sucking and biting at the exact spot where her neck met shoulder, Madison, who cruelly used the peppermint soap, knowing it would burn, counting on that, to open her up, to penetrate her.

Madison, who made her scream, over and over again.

"Hurt me," she begged and Madison was more than happy to oblige.

CHAPTER TEN

Hurt me. She started her second book with those very words. Hurt me. Like a prayer. Natasha closes her eyes and lets her head drop to her chest, her dark hair a veil around her face. She rarely thinks about Madison, but when she does, it's always with quiet fondness. Madison. The perfect dream girl: kinky, smart, beautiful.

Looking back, Natasha can't help but wonder if Madison was the one who opened that door, fomenting those dark desires that until then, Natasha had believed existed only in the world of fantasy. With Madison, she found her perfect counterpart, the natural pairing. Top – bottom. Dominant – submissive. Sadist – masochist. Those words were never used, but they hovered at the periphery, unnecessary in the face of the obvious.

She never worried about crossing the line. Of asking for something that would scare her off. Madison, with her mischievous little smile, would look at her and say, "Your wish is my command."

Their relationship was organic. Later, as she dug deeper

into the world she wrote about, Natasha read all about detailed contracts between lovers, safe words and the painstaking process of cataloguing all that is or is not permissible. With Madison, everything was permissible. She never asked for permission and she didn't have to because Natasha knew, always, that if she said stop, Madison would.

Something tells her that with Adam, things wouldn't be so simple. What she shared with Madison was rare, special, an exploration only possible for the young, protected in their innocence, in their belief that a person who loves you would never truly hurt you.

But she is no longer twenty-five and Adam, with his perfect face and his quiet power, strikes her as a man who would leave nothing to chance. A man who would demand from her acceptance long before an act occurred.

The thought, for the first time ever, arouses her.

What would it be like, she wonders, to be with someone experienced in kink? Not that she isn't experienced, but her experience has always felt unsure. The experience of a novice. And her knowledge comes as much from researching books as it does from actual experience.

Adam has the look of an expert.

And she has always wondered what a difference that would make. What secrets he knows, what tricks he has learned, to make everything all that more intense?

She hates that she can't stop thinking about him. That he has dug his way into her brain. She doesn't want to hear the echo of his words in her mind. Doesn't want to imagine him stripping her, digging his strong fingers into her flesh, bruising her, delighting her, hurting her until she's wet with desire.

If she believed in god, she might have thought he'd dropped Adam in her life to tempt her. To test her. That serpent in the tree, designed just for her.

When she left the apartment earlier, she saw the hurt in Christopher's eyes. He wanted her to stay, though he never said it. He never has to. Work is work and he knows that better than anyone. Knows the difficulty of balancing teaching and writing, of making time. That it isn't a luxury but a necessity. That she has only six years to prove herself to the university, six years to publish and teach and appear on panels and discussions so they grant her tenure.

Otherwise, they'll terminate her contract.

But it's been a long time since Christopher had to worry about such things. His position is solid. His reputation sterling. He is able to take long weekends, to relax, to sit back and let other people take the spotlight. As much as he understands, does he really remember what it was like?

So she fled. Hailed a taxi and went to the studio so she can be alone. Except with her mind racing and thoughts of Adam, she isn't alone.

In front of her, the blank page with its blinking cursor stares back, taunting her.

Hurt me. Make me bleed. Make me suffer.

Oh, how she wants to suffer. Call it masochism of the least satisfying variety. Emotional masochism. The masochism where no one gets off and everyone just suffers. So she opens the word document labeled *Blackmailed* and she writes about suffering. Delicious, torturous suffering, knowing it's a mistake, one she will not be able to undo.

With one hand she types while her other hand moves over her body, a soft caress, the hint of suggestion, enough to make her nipples hard. The staccato banging of the keyboard is swallowed up by Brahms.

Her fingers slip lower, sliding beneath her lace panties. Natasha isn't a woman with expensive tastes, but when it comes to lingerie, she sees no reason to hold back. She has the money. Why not spend it.

She strokes her sex, feeling her arousal on her fingertips, and closes her eyes, letting the scene come to life.

She stands naked before him in a large, airy bathroom. Black and white tiles and a claw foot tub. He tells her to lean against the vanity, her legs spread wide, her hands gripping the cool marble.

The chill in the air makes her nipples hard. Painfully hard. He pulls a chair in front of her and sits with his legs wide apart and his elbows resting on his knees and stares at her pussy.

"You have such a magnificent cunt," he whispers as he runs one elegant finger down her slit, finding her wet. He nudges her lips apart, letting his finger slide slowly into her sex.

"It's a pity to hide it under all this hair."

He reaches around her, and she knows what's coming, the old-fashioned shaving set. Not once does he ask for permission. He doesn't have to. He owns her. With an expert hand, he lathers her completely with the rough bristled brush. A tingle of fear runs down her spine when she sees the flashing blade of the straight razor in his hand.

"Stand still. I don't want to hurt you."

Her pussy tightens and she takes quick, shallow breaths. She watches as he flicks the blade over her, slicing easily through her hair, stripping her bare.

He moves slowly. Carefully. It takes an eternity but when he's done, she is completely naked. Not a hair in sight. She's dripping with desire.

He washes away the traces of soap with a damp washcloth and she trembles, the adrenaline heightening every sensation.

When he slips his finger into her, the sensation is exquisite and he makes a sound deep in his throat, conveying his pleasure. She clenches around his finger. Just that single finger, unmoving, is almost enough to make her come.

"That's how your pussy should look. Always. And if it isn't to my liking, I will punish you. Severely."

"Yes, sir." Her trembling voice echoes through the tiled room. Fear. Submission. Arousal. Promise. She believes him, knowing that his words are less a threat and more a promise.

He will mark her. Hurt her. He may even make her bleed.

And the thought, though terrifying, makes her wet.

"Can I come?" she asks hoarsely.

He shakes his head. "After the way you've teased me, I don't think you should be allowed to come, do you?"

She swallows hard. "Please?"

"You're beautiful when you beg."

"I'll do anything. Please."

He laughs cruelly. "You teased me. Now it's your turn to suffer."

He withdraws his hand and comes to his feet, pressing his fingers to her lips. She opens her mouth obediently, tasting her arousal on his skin. Wordlessly, he unzips his pants, freeing his beautiful erection, hard and thick and perfect and she licks her lips before sinking to her knees.

"Spread your legs wider. I want to see your bare cunt while you suck me off."

When she doesn't move fast enough, he kicks her legs open and she has to brace herself on the floor to keep from falling over. She rights herself and then she opens her mouth wide and accepts every inch of him, letting him gag her with his magnificent erection. She can feel the tears at the corners of her eyes, threatening to spill.

Her body begs for release. The taste of his cock makes her sex drip.

"That's it. That's my good little fuck slave."

Her chest swells with pride and she opens her mouth, taking him as deep as he will go.

Natasha sits back, cheeks flushed, eyes glassy and closes the computer screen. Enough. She has had enough. She can't do this. Can't conduct an affair, even if it's only on paper. She's made Christopher no promises, but some promises do not need to be made with words.

And she has promised Christopher, through a thousand tiny acts, that she is his and only his.

She's proud of what she's done. What she's accomplished. The little self-published smut empire that is hers and only hers and she wishes, sometimes, that she could share it with him, that she could make him understand. But she knows that if she told him, even if he never said the words aloud, she'd see them written across his face.

Why are you wasting your talent on this?

Her silk robe is damp and her body begs for release, her arousal tightening like a noose.

Sure, her days are often filled with making edits — a comma splice is a comma splice, no matter what you're writing. But when she's doing this, when she's inventing, creating, she often walks away from her computer shaky with need.

The words in the story echo in her mind, his voice so

real it's as if he's actually here with her.

I don't think you should be allowed to come, do you?

She shudders, the muscles of her abdomen rippling, a wave of pleasure without even being touching. It isn't orgasm denial that leaves her panting, it's the way he makes her party to her own suffering, the way he makes her agree.

She shakes her head, knowing she will never be able to publish this. Not when Adam knows who she is.

So why waste her time?

But she knows the answer. All she has to do is think about him, about his face, about his body, about his muscular forearms with their tattoos, tattoos she'd do anything to see. But she won't. She can't.

That's why she's wasting her time.

The blind hope that maybe, just maybe, by writing about it she can exorcise her desire.

Her legs tremble when she stands and walks towards the bed, mentally going over the contents of her toy box, the bullet vibrator she sometimes inserts into her pussy when she's writing, just to keep things interesting, the bejeweled glass butt plug that's both playful and cruel, the whips and paddles and floggers, but at the last second, just as she's about to open it, she lets her hand fall by her side. Turning away, she grabs her clothing off the floor and gets dressed. Replacing the layers that will make her whole again outside this room.

Christopher is waiting. It isn't fair to make him wait any longer.

After all, it isn't an orgasm she's after. Orgasms, though marvelous, are cheap and easy. A physical reaction to stimuli. No, what she craves is stickier, more complicated.

What she craves cannot be achieved in a quarter of an hour before dinner.

You're going to regret this, she thinks, laughing at herself.

And then, just to be a little crueler, she opens the toy box and selects a pair of metal ben wa balls, the heaviest set she owns, the ones with the little weighted bells inside that ring together every time they strike, sending vibrations through her sex.

They slide in easily, the cold metal a shocking contrast to her burning heat.

With that she heads to the door. What's the fun of depriving yourself if you don't make things a little more difficult, she thinks, locking up her studio and heading home.

CHAPTER ELEVEN

Christopher pauses to sip his wine as he puts the finishing touches on dinner. Natasha leans against the door, admiring him in silence. There's something so unexpected and erotic about his passion for cooking. Once, when they first started dating, he asked how such a sensual woman could be so indifferent to cooking. She didn't have an answer for him then. And now, watching him, she realizes she still has no answer except that she is impatient.

Christopher turns, giving her such a surprised smile, like he didn't really think she'd come home, even though they have plans, that it knocks the air from her lungs.

"Hey," she says, suddenly shy. Every step she takes makes the balls inside her click together, the vibrations shooting through her, that low level of excitement, that drives her crazy, delicious waves, gentle, sensual, inescapable. Wrapping her arms around his neck, she kisses him.

"I thought about you all day." The lie feels true the

moment she says it. In the cab on the way home, she imagined all the things she'd do once she saw him. There, in the back seat of the taxi, as upper Manhattan passed by in a blur of brownstones, she slipped her hand under her skirt, touching her wet pussy, teasing herself as she thought about Christopher, about his cock, about him inside of her.

She didn't care if the driver saw. Even then, it felt like a dream. Surreal. Without consequences.

Natasha takes the wine glass from him, sipping the icy cold white wine before returning it with a wicked smile.

"Dinner will be ready in a minute," he says but she just shakes her head, keeping her eyes locked on Christopher as she slowly drops to her knees in the middle of the kitchen.

"Dinner can wait." She unzips his pants and watches the protest drain from his face. With an impatient gesture, he reaches over her and flips off the burner on the stove before settling back on his heels. His cock, now free, is hard and ready.

With one final glance at Christopher, she cups his balls and runs her tongue along the entire length of him, tasting him, savoring him. She wants to please him. Wants to make him lose control.

He inhales sharply as her lips close around him, taking him deep into her mouth, sucking him gently as she snakes one hand between her thighs, feeling her wet sex. She strokes herself as she lavishes attention on Christopher's erection, letting her own pleasure vibrate down her throat. Her tongue darts out, tickling the base of his cock and he groans, his cock twitching with pleasure. With sudden fierceness, he grips her hair, his fingers digging into her scalp as he forces her head back so she can see him. In his face, she sees raw, fierce desire that only intensifies the pulsing need between her legs.

She wants the oblivion of their union. She wants the oblivion of the flesh, bodies joined as the world around ceases to exist.

She sucks him deeper, harder, stronger, her fingers on her clit picking up speed as she rocks on her knees, bringing herself closer. The image flashes in her head. A woman bowing in prayer.

As much as she loves to feel him come in her mouth, she wants him to fuck her. With one final wet, hungry suck, she releases his cock and comes to her feet. Her legs tremble. She doesn't undress. Pulling her skirt up around her waist, she yanks down her panties as Christopher watches on and then with a quick tug, she yanks the ben wa balls from her cunt, letting them drop noisily to the floor.

With one last wicked smile, she turns around, resting her forearms on the counter and her head on her forearms, and pushes her ass up.

His hands are on her, gripping her hips, lifting them higher as his erection presses against her wet folds.

He penetrates her slowly, easing into her when all she wants is one brutal thrust to push her over the edge. She pushes back but he keeps his hands on her hips, limiting her movements, making her his prisoner.

She moans in frustration as Christopher kisses her neck, sending a fresh wave of desire spiraling through her. Her toes curl.

"You're so wet," he moans, still only half-way inside her, still tormenting her with his ability to hold back.

"I couldn't stop thinking about you. About this."

"Tell me what you were thinking."

"I thought about you hurting me," she whispers into her arms, thankful that she can't see his expression. Nothing scares her more than the idea of one day going too far and Christopher looking at her with revulsion and disgust.

"You want me to hurt you?" His cock twitches and she knows, now is not that moment.

"Yes."

He thrusts into her and she cries out in surprise. "Yes!"

He pulls out, making her heart stop, and then thrusts back into her, yanking another passionate cry from her lips. His fingers bruise her hips.

"I thought about you hitting me so hard I had bruises for a week." She sighs with pleasure as he eases out of her, his body crushing her against the cold surface of the counter. "Hurt me," she begs. "Hurt me, please."

His low growl makes her shiver. She doesn't expect it. And when his palm lands on her ass, her pussy tightens around his cock, pulling him deeper.

"Again," she moans.

He pounds into her, hitting her with his palm between thrusts, the sound of their bodies crashing together, the sound of his hand against her flesh music to her ears.

"Harder," she begs, lost in pleasure. For a moment, she forgets where she is. Who she's with. All she knows is that she needs this. Her body needs this. Her mind needs this. He fucks her like it's the last thing he will ever do, fucks her hard as she bites her lip to stop from screaming.

She nearly laughs, imagining what their elderly neighbors must be thinking if they can hear them now.

She feels like she's flying. And when Christopher delivers one final blow before burying himself inside her, moaning like an animal as he comes, hips bucking, she loses control, screaming out, her orgasm ripping her apart as she grips the tiled counter until her knuckles turn white.

He sags into her, his weight crushing her against the counter as they pant together, his cock still twitching inside her.

With a final gentle kiss to her neck, Christopher eases out of her, setting off a final wave of aftershocks.

She doesn't notice the marks on her hips until she turns around. The crescent moons dotted with blood from where Christopher's nails broke her skin. She pushes her skirt down, but it's too late.

Christopher's heart wrenching expression.

"Oh god, Natasha, I am so sorry." His eyes wide with regret. She knows that expression. He's asking himself how he let it go so far.

She tastes the sickness at the back of her throat, bile. Not because of what he did, but because of how it makes him feel.

"It's okay. I'm okay. I promise." She tries to soothe him, knowing just how useless it is. The image, those tiny crescent moons, will haunt him. She sees it in his eyes, the way he can't look away.

"It's okay, I promise," she insists, knowing this time, she went too far.

Whatever pleasure she felt is gone. She looks around, only now realizing where they are. The kitchen. Dinner on the stove.

She wants to tell him that he couldn't hurt her even if he tried. Instead, she turns, smiling up at his beautiful, concerned face and brushes his hair back with her fingers. "You didn't hurt me. That was wonderful."

The moment she says it, she realizes it was the wrong thing to say. She wants to kiss him until the look in his eyes is gone. Wants to protect him. From her.

He is her world. And she is his. Looking at him, it scares her. It's too much for one person. Too much to ask of anyone.

CHAPTER TWELVE

They met at a coffee shop with a red awning and a menu written in chalk on a giant board behind the counter. It wasn't the type of place Natasha would normally go with its organic selection of teas and cold brew coffee and outside, at bistro tables lining the sidewalk, women who looked like models, their tiny dogs panting beneath the tables.

When Christopher arrived, he looked the same and yet so different from how she remembered him. He was just as handsome, but instead of shorts and t-shirts, he was wearing jeans and a white oxford, the top two buttons undone, the sleeves pushed up so she could see the golden hairs on his arm. He smiled at her, one of those genuine, delighted smiles and ordered a tea then paused and asked what she wanted. She glanced at the menu, glanced at Christopher, felt guilty about him paying and knowing that he would insist.

"A large black iced coffee."

He pointed to a blueberry scone and then pulled his

wallet from his back pocket, his thick wrist, his marvelous fingers, and waved away her offer to pay.

"We aren't in the kind of relationship where you pay for things like coffee," he said with such assurance, she could only stare at him as she struggled to decode the meaning of his words.

They waited for their drinks, each second standing next to him making Natasha's anxiety spike, and then they went outside, sitting on the rickety metal chairs, and Natasha felt the hot metal digging into her thighs, sticky with sweat.

Christopher smiled again as he looked at her. There was no embarrassment. No shame. Just interest. And Natasha couldn't quite determine if it was sexual interest or something else. Something stickier, trickier to identify.

"I'm glad you called."

"Texted."

He shrugged. "It's all the same." He broke off a piece of the scone, the large crystals of sugar on the top glistening in the sun, and offered it to her. She shook her head, which made him smile again. He deposited it into his mouth and chewed and she loved the way he chewed, thoughtful, careful, like a giant cow. Meditative.

"When you get to be my age, you realize it's not worth playing games. I'm selfish. I want the things I want and I'm not ashamed to admit that." He broke off another piece of scone and Natasha leaned forward, pulse racing, heart beating in her chest. "I want you. And I'll do whatever it takes to make you mine." He spoke clearly, without guile, without remorse. A man stating facts rather than emotions or desires. "It's over between me and Elsa. She moved out."

Sitting beneath the lush trees in Greenwich Village,

Natasha had no idea how much those words would change her life.

They talked for hours and then, at the subway, he squeezed her hand, that was it, just a gentle squeeze of her hand, and it made her heart race like nothing else. "Take all the time you need. I'll wait."

CHAPTER THIRTEEN

His certainty that day at the coffee shop didn't scare her. It aroused her. Amazed her. Astounded her, but it never scared her.

Now his certainty terrifies her. Then, there was nothing to lose. There was only the magical possibility of what might be.

Four years later and the words that once filled her with excitement, I'll wait, feel instead like the executioner's garrote, slowly tightening, slowly cutting off her air supply. I'll wait. A ticking time bomb.

Wiping the semen from her thighs, she stares at her reflection in the mirror, angling her body so she can see the red handprints on her ass and the crescent moons left by his nails. The handprints are already beginning to fade, and by the time she gets into bed later, they'll be gone completely.

She shivers, dropping the damp toilet paper in the trash. Forever is a long time.

Whenever she thinks about the future, she can't shake

the sensation that it's hurtling towards her like a train on a collision course.

She knows, implicitly, what it holds. The details are changeable, but the picture remains the same. Marriage. Children. Relinquishing herself to another.

If she could, she would live in this moment forever. The simple comfort of their lives as they are now. But such a thing is impossible. She may as well be wishing for the pot of gold at the end of the rainbow.

She washes her hands, soaps away the smell of sex, of their bodies, the smell she loves, the smell Christopher would object to while they sit together at the dining room table, eating the meal he's prepared.

Sex, to Christopher, belongs in the bedroom. It belongs between the sheets of a bed. Contained. The bedroom isn't a physical space so much as it's an idea. Separate from the rest of their lives. It doesn't mean he won't fuck her anywhere he can – Christopher is, and has always been, a very sexual man. But there's no blurring of lines for him.

She can't shake the feeling that somewhere along the way she's made a wrong turn. She experiences this often in her writing, the moment where she realizes the story has fallen flat because of a decision made twenty pages earlier, the wrong decision, and everything that follows is diminished as a result.

In writing, it's easy to pinpoint the place, to rectify the situation with a quick stroke of keys. Copy. Delete. And then the freedom of the blank page. The freedom to do as she pleases. To change her mind. To revise.

Some moments are pivotal. A moment in a café in Greenwich Village. A moment, in bed, picking up a cell phone and deciding to call. Moments that seem so trivial at the time. Later, you look back and realize, that's when everything changed.

She pulls her messy, well-fucked hair into a ponytail and leaves the bathroom, smiling though she doesn't feel like smiling anymore. And when she gets to the dining room, the plates are already set on the table and Christopher is sipping a glass of wine, looking so damn civilized, so damn perfect. He won't mention what happened in the kitchen. Won't say a word about how he's feeling. For the next thirty minutes, they'll eat dinner and talk about the minutia of their lives apart, like so many dinners before and so many dinners to come.

But Natasha, staring at her plate, doesn't want pleasant or civilized. She doesn't want silence or the resentments seething beneath the surface

As she picks up her knife and fork, she wants to throw a glass at the wall just to watch it shatter. Wants to light the apartment on fire and step back to watch the carnage unfold.

She glances at her already filled glass of wine, knowing she shouldn't drink it. That when she's in one of these moods, it's best to stay sober and wait for it to pass.

She smiles at Christopher. "This looks amazing," she says, meaning it. And then she picks up her wine and takes a sip.

CHAPTER FOURTEEN

After dinner, as Christopher piles their dishes into the dishwasher, Natasha texts Maggie. *Free for a drink?*

The sane and rational part of her hopes Maggie's already safely back in Brooklyn and that she'll be forced to give up on the thought of going out, of having one too many drinks, of forgetting about her life.

But moments later, when her phone chirps in her hand, it's Maggie, saying she's still on campus and suggesting they meet at The Mark in half an hour.

Natasha glances at Christopher, so calmly putting away dishes, humming to himself. The guilt rises up inside her, nauseating and she pushes it back down, refusing to give in, refusing to feel guilty when she's done nothing wrong.

See you there.

The bar is crowded, but somehow, Maggie was able to get their usual corner booth. She's reading despite the dim light and the noise, her head bowed as she squints at the page in front of her.

"Anything good?" Natasha slides into the booth.

Maggie grimaces, slamming the book shut. "Not even a little." Her eyes narrow and Natasha can feel her sizing her up, checking for cracks and fissures before finally she says, "What's wrong?"

Natasha once read that women are more attuned to pick up minute emotional tells, the nonverbal forms of communication, than men, making it easier to speak without fully formed sentences, to intuit. To simply know.

Now, in the shadowy bar, she doesn't know if this is a curse or a blessing. She's so tired of lying. Of half-truths told just to get through the day. She wants to tell her everything.

Say it, the voice screams in Natasha's head. *Say it. Tell her. Tell her everything.*

And she almost does.

"Don't tell me, Christopher is already pestering you about kids," Maggie jokes, her smile freezing when she sees the look on Natasha's face. "Oh fuck."

Natasha thinks about Christopher's hand on her belly as they sleep, side by side, the sensation at the base of her neck saying that he is imagining her pregnant, imagining her carrying his child.

"No, nothing like that." Maggie raises one eyebrow skeptically and Natasha adds, "He hasn't said anything, at least. But I can tell that he's thinking about it."

"How old is he now?" Maggie leans forward, her elbows resting on the sticky surface of the table.

"He turns fifty next year."

She whistles.

"I just feel lost, you know? Like maybe I'm not doing what I should be doing?"

"What should you be doing?"

"I have no fucking idea. Sometimes I think I'm just not cut out of monogamy." Natasha bites her lip. It's the truth. Sort of. Mostly the truth, though only a small piece.

"Recent studies have debunked the long held theory that monogamy is natural," Maggie says slowly. "Apparently, the original studies were seriously flawed and designed just to reaffirm the status quo."

"Thanks, that's really reassuring."

"All I'm saying is, it's natural. To have doubts. You've been together, what? Five years?"

"Four."

"Fine, four years. You're well past the exciting, everything is new, everything is magical phase. Now you're in the, whenever I close my eyes I can see us sitting together on a porch is some small town, sixty years down the line. It's scary."

"Really?"

Maggie shrugs. "What the hell do I know? I keep going back to the same douche bag who can't commit for more than thirty seconds."

Natasha laughs, sipping her whiskey through the straw. "How is dear old Marco?"

"Who the fuck knows? I haven't heard from him since this summer, which basically means he's banging his new TA." Natasha sees the pain behind Maggie's casual shrug. She wishes there were something she could say but they both know Marco is never going to change. To think otherwise is just cruel.

Natasha, perhaps buoyed by the whiskey in her glass, perhaps by the feeling that everything is changing, faster than she can stop it, faster than she wants, blurts out the words before she can think twice about it.

"Have you ever heard of Layla Allen?"

Maggie frowns, pressing her lips together. "That erotica writer?" she asks finally, confused. "Never read her. That seems more like your sort of thing."

"What makes you say that?"

Maggie laughs. "Are you fucking joking? Jesus woman, I've never met anyone who thinks about sex more than you."

Natasha laughs nervously. All she has to do is say it. That's it. Maggie's her friend. Maggie's always going to be her friend. And Maggie would never, in a million years, let her secret slip to someone at the university.

She looks up and her mouth shuts quickly when she sees him pushing through the crowd of people, moving towards the bar. Holding on to his arm and following in his wake is Amanda, the blond girl from the Poetry Fellows cocktail hour.

Whatever Natasha was about to say is forgotten as a hot wash of jealously hits her.

CHAPTER FIFTEEN

Adam slips past groups of people like they don't exist, making his way to the bar, Amanda close on his heels. Natasha keeps her head down, silently hoping that he won't spot her. But when his eyes sweep over her, she feels it, her skin tightening. When their eyes meet across the room, he lifts his hand, indicating he'll be over in a minute.

Natasha sinks lower into the booth.

"So, you want to spice things up? Get a little wild and crazy? I have to say, Christopher doesn't seem like the type."

Natasha looks up in confusion.

"Layla Allen," Maggie adds when she sees Natasha's expression.

"If I tell you something, will you promise not to tell anyone? And I mean, anyone."

Maggie sits up, her interest piqued. "Yeah, of course."

"I'm Layla Allen."

The silence is deafening despite the noise that encircles

them. Natasha, biting her lip, waits for Maggie's reaction, fearing the worst.

But what's the worst?

For once, Maggie is at a loss for words. She stares at her, dumbfounded. "Are you fucking kidding?"

"I will cut you if you tell anyone."

Maggie slaps the table, laughing. "Holy hell." She leans back, looking at Natasha in a new light. "Well, good for you." She raises her glass as she shakes her head, still laughing. "Jesus Christ, I can't believe you didn't tell me. Why didn't you tell me?"

Natasha shrugs. "I didn't tell anyone."

"Not even Christopher?"

"Especially not Christopher."

Maggie pulls at her lower lip. "Yeah, I guess that makes sense."

"What does?"

"I don't know. He's just so…traditional sometimes." Maggie shrugs. "I don't mean that in a bad way. It's just…I don't know. But I can understand why you might want to keep it from him."

Natasha sags with relief. "You're not upset?"

"Why, because you didn't tell me?" Maggie makes a face. "Don't be an idiot. If anyone finds out, kiss tenure goodbye. Secret's safe with me."

"Thank you."

"So, now I want all the gory details. They're all BDSM books, right? Like whips and chains and sex toys I've never even heard of." Maggie grins and her infectious enthusiasm makes Natasha laugh along with her.

"You don't even want to know some of the things I've seen."

"Oh, I most certainly do."

"Ever heard of CBT?"

Maggie's brow furrows. "Cognitive behavior therapy?"

Natasha, now grinning, shakes her head. "No. Cock and ball torture."

Maggie's eyes go wide. "More please."

Natasha, thinking of one particularly gruesome spiked metal cock ring she once saw while researching a book, opens her mouth as a shadow falls over their table. When she looks up, Adam is looming over her, his dark eyes glittering. For a moment, he just watches her and Natasha's heart begins to race.

"We haven't met," he says, turning to Maggie with an outstretched hand. "Adam LaRue."

"He's in my intro to fiction workshop."

"A little old to be a freshman, aren't you?"

"Second year. Poetry. I'm just auditing. Thought it would be fun."

Maggie leans back, drinking him in. "Come on, sit," she says finally, taking her eyes off Adam long enough to include Amanda. "You're never going to find a table."

Maggie gives Natasha a look that says, we aren't even close to done talking about this, before shifting her attention to Amanda.

"You're a poet also?"

Amanda nods and Maggie clasps her hands together.

"Fantastic. I adore poets. Entertain me. Writing programs are like soap operas except everyone is a little more homely and significantly more intelligent." Maggie frowns before correcting herself. "Most people are somewhat more intelligent and significantly more homely."

When Adam laughs, sliding into the booth next to

Natasha, she can feel the deep rumble move through her chest. Amanda, with a nervous glance towards him, slips into the seat next to Maggie.

"Divorces? Affairs? Come on. There were thirty people in my MFA class and by the time we finished, three were divorced, two got married, and one person had a nervous breakdown and ended up in a loony bin out in the sticks. Don't tell me you're that dreaded boring year − all happy childhoods and babies and sickening flowers."

"I always thought poets were the crazy ones," Adam says, chuckling. "Apparently, I was misinformed."

"Oh, fiction writers are out of their minds. Terrible occupational hazard."

"Tendency towards megalomania, depression and a passion for substance abuse," Natasha deadpans, lifting her glass of bourbon.

"Pathological need for attention," Maggie adds.

"It's the sexual frustration. Sexless adolescence. Sickeningly pale skin. Makes them go mad."

Even as the words pour out of her, easy, light, she knows it's a mistake. It feels too easy. Too simple. The edges blur and the boundaries shift and she just lets it. She keeps her eyes on Maggie, afraid of what might happen if she glances over at Adam.

And then he does it. He brushes his thigh against hers, jean clad thigh against jean clad thigh and it sends a tingle running down her spine, that awareness of his body making her heart race just a little faster.

When he moves his leg away, she chews her lip in disappointment.

"So, you really have no stories for me?" Maggie sits back, crestfallen. "Kids these days. So respectable. So boring."

Amanda sits rigidly in her seat, her drink untouched on the table and Natasha wonders, suddenly, if she is one of the casualties they're so cavalierly joking about. One of the ones who started out shiny and happy and perhaps even married and now, a year and a half later, is trying, unsuccessfully, to pick up the pieces of her shattered life.

Natasha can relate to.

The pounding bass makes it difficult to hear and when Maggie leans over, saying something to Amanda, the words are swallowed up in the din. Adam takes that moment to lean in close, so only she can hear him and whisper, "I like her. Fiery. Tell me, have you two ever...?"

Natasha turns sharply, glaring at him while he grins back at her.

"Don't tell me you've never thought about it?"

"So, how's the book coming?" Natasha asks, turning back to Maggie.

She groans. "Mention it again and I *will* stab you."

"Right, point taken."

When Adam's hand grazes her thigh, she thinks she's mistaken, but then he does it again and her spine stiffens. Even through the fabric of her jeans, the heat of his palm is inescapable. Her mouth goes dry as she tries, unsuccessfully, to ignore him. To ignore the sensation of his thumb tracing slow circles on her thigh, daring her to stop him. To ignore the way she feels his touch all the way to her sex.

She stares straight ahead, trying to ignore the riot of sensations that thumb is causing her. But as much as she wants him to remove it, she wants him to keep touching her just as much.

Torn, divided, she tries to act normal. Tries to ignore his sensual caresses. Tries to pay attention to what Maggie is saying, but it's like her ears are filled with cotton. All she hears is the rush of blood, the pulsing bass, the haze of far away conversations.

Adam's hand dances across her leg, and her nipples harden.

She is suddenly aware of every part of her body. The heat between her legs. The place where her shoulders meet the sticky vinyl booth.

As his hand slides slowly up her thigh, she parts her legs on instinct, letting his long, able fingers continue their slow progress upward.

"How long have you known each other?" he asks, casually resting one elbow on the table as he addresses Maggie, his hand continuing its teasing exploration.

"Since Nat started teaching. So what, three years?" Maggie looks to Natasha who can only nod her head, afraid of what may accidentally come out if she tries to speak.

She imagines his hand, higher, closer, deftly unbuttoning her jeans as they sit in the corner booth.

Her cheeks burn.

Natasha lifts her drink, desperate to appear normal. His fingers dance upward then retreat, returning to her knee, swirling patterns on her skin. Then up again, teasing, higher this time, closer to her pussy.

She chokes, coughing as whiskey burns down the wrong pipe. She wipes her mouth with the back of her hand as everyone stares at her.

"Are you okay?"

"I'm fine. I just need the bathroom. Anyone want

anything while I'm up?"

"Another round."

Adam gives her thigh one last squeeze, hard enough that she feels it all the way in her pussy, and then he withdraws, sliding out of the booth to make room for her to get out.

The bathrooms are in the back, hidden from view by a false wall, giving the illusion of privacy in a room crowded with bodies. Natasha leans her head against the wall, closing her eyes.

What the hell is she doing?

Secretly, she hopes Adam will follow her. The way he touched under the table, indifferent to the people around them.

It wasn't carelessness. It was confidence.

Keeping her eyes closed, she loses herself in the delicious fantasy. He'd be on her the moment she opens the door, pushing her into the bathroom roughly, spinning her around and kissing her hard on the mouth.

It's the allure of bar bathrooms. Chance encounters. Brief, passionate couplings. The type of quick, dirty fuck fueled by alcohol and desperation. Clawing fingers. A need so potent it can bring you to your knees.

Palms flat on the mirror as his long, lean body presses into her. Watching him rip off her panties and then stretch her open with his fingers, stroking and teasing.

The heat between her legs, just thinking about it, leaves her dizzy.

She's ready. She was ready before he lay a hand on her. He withdraws his fingers, his cock poised at her pussy, and then, with one brutal thrust that shoves her forward, he fills her. His expression in the bathroom mirror, possessive, arrogant, haughty as he wraps one hand around her throat, his fingers tightening enough to make her know he's serious. His fingers on her clit as he steadily fucks her, watching her get closer and closer in the mirror, watching her eyes glaze over, her expression lost, her mouth hanging open as she whimpers.

Someone taps her shoulder and Natasha's eyes fly open. She looks around, surprised to find she's still waiting for the bathroom. A girl motions to the door and Natasha slips inside, bolting the door quickly behind her.

The heat between her legs makes her foolish and reckless. Natasha doesn't care about the people waiting for the bathroom. She slides her hand into her jeans, feeling her pussy, wet and hot and engorged. When she touches her clit, she jumps.

She leans against the wall, watching her reflection in the mirror above the sink. Watching the color come to her cheeks. Watching the wide-eyed stare. She rubs her clit harder, the pleasure coursing through her fast and steady. It won't take much. Just this. Just seeing this. Just watching herself in the mirror. Just thinking about him.

Her mouth twists into a silent scream as she climaxes, forcing her eyes to remain locked on the image in the mirror as she rides the waves of her orgasm. With one final shudder, she slips her hand out of her jeans, and unable to resist the urge, licks her fingers.

Quickly, she uses the bathroom and leaves, passing the girl waiting on line with a smile before heading straight for the bar. She leans against the scuffed wood, the scent of her arousal still filling her nostrils, and orders another round.

Adam takes one look at her, at the easy roll of her hips

and her flushed cheeks and gives her a knowing smile, which she ignores, feeling emboldened by her orgasm. She studies him, the sharp angular lines of his face, the stubble along his jaw. Natasha realizes, as she sips her drink, that she feels powerful. His desire, so clear on his face, isn't a threat. It's power. She was wrong to be afraid of it.

When Maggie suggests they play darts, Natasha reluctantly leaves the booth and the protection it offers, the possibility of Adam's hand once more on her thigh, the possibility of more stolen caresses.

They form two teams. Maggie and Natasha against Amanda and Adam. Adam leans against the bar as Natasha steadies herself, one eye closed as she focuses on the target.

She pulls back then lets the dart fly.

Maggie claps wildly and Natasha turns, smiling and bowing slightly.

"I'm beginning to regret betting the next round on this game," Adam says, going to retrieve the darts from their tight cluster around the bull's-eye.

"Sore loser?" Natasha jokes and Adam glances over his shoulder at her, his eyes playful, mysterious.

"Oh, I never lose."

That cockiness, which on anyone else would have made Natasha groan, instead leaves her anxious for more.

"You're in Christopher's workshop, right?" she asks, turning away from Adam.

Amanda looks at her in surprise before finally answering. "Yeah, we both are." She points her thumb at Adam, who has just landed his final dart a few millimeters from the center of the target.

"How's it going?"

"I love it," she beams. "Christopher's amazing." The girl blushes, making her look suddenly much younger. "Obviously, you already know that."

"He is definitely that," Natasha agrees.

Maggie's laughing at something Adam is saying, yanking the darts out of his hand, and for a second, Natasha forgets Christopher, forgets lesson plans and the pressure to write her next book, and sips her beer, feeling like she is back in grad school, when all she ever had to worry about was reading and writing. Normally, when she thinks about that time of her life, she feels only creeping dread, but there were fun times, also. Times when she enjoyed herself. Playing darts and drinking beer, she is reminded of those moments. And then, at the end of the night, as they all piled into the street, laughing, drunk, stumbling, and she'd wave goodbye before getting on the L train and heading back home. Sometimes alone.

But often not.

It wasn't all bad.

Amanda has class in the morning, so she leaves after the first round of darts. They laugh and joke and play and then it's Maggie who is saying she has to leave. Living in Brooklyn, she's at the fickle mercy of the subways. Natasha offers up her couch, even though she knows Christopher will be mad if he finds Maggie asleep there in the morning, but Maggie shakes her head, saying she'd rather wake up in her own bed.

They leave together, the three of them stepping into the quiet evening.

If they were younger, if things were different, this would be the moment when someone, right before they got to the train, suggested just one last drink. An excuse to prolong the night. To put off going home a little longer. She half expects someone to suggest it, the night feels that much like the past. But then the train is coming and Maggie is darting down the stairs and out of sight.

Natasha stands alone next to Adam on the wide deserted sidewalk and wonders how she got here. How this is her life.

Beneath the street lamps, Adam looks older, more serious, his face drawn as if he's trying to come up with the answer to a complicated problem and whatever confidence she felt at the bar wavers under his searching gaze.

She wants something from him, something she can't have and it's maddening. And yet, she loves the feeling. The excitement. The newness. The possibility. Isn't that what it is? The realization that she has no idea what is about to happen. That the story has yet to be written.

If he kisses her, will she sink into him or push him away, slapping him hard across the face?

There's no way of knowing. And Natasha is old enough to know that nothing could possibly compete with the exhilarating feeling of the unknown.

"I'll walk you home," Adam says gruffly, starting off in the direction of her apartment without waiting for her response.

Their feet slap the pavement, echoing, filling the silence. The occasional car speeds down the street before disappearing around the corner. In the quiet, Natasha's thoughts grow louder.

The answerless questions.

She watches Adam out of the corner of her eye, silently willing him to speak, but his gaze remains locked on the sidewalk before him, his silence an impenetrable wall when all she wants is to know what he's thinking. When they approach Morningside Park, he stops abruptly and sits on a park bench, pulling a pack of cigarettes out and lighting one. Natasha sits next to him, acutely aware of the space between them on the seat. She wants his thigh against hers. But more than that, she wants him to be the one to initiate such a touch.

He smokes in silence, staring out across the intersection as the streetlights change from red to green and back again. The voice in her head screams, *say something!*, but every time Natasha opens her mouth, she closes it again without uttering a word.

Whatever happened in the bar, the moment is clearly over. The thought makes her heart sink, though she knows she should be relieved. A bullet dodged.

But she isn't ready to let go of the excitement. For one night, she wants to feel alive. For one night, she wants that old feeling back, that excitement and unknowing.

Eventually, Adam drops his cigarette to the ground, stubbing it out beneath the heel of his scuffed Converse. She expects him to get up, to walk the final block and a half to her apartment building, Christopher's apartment building.

Instead, he turns to her, his eyes gleaming in the darkness.

Kiss me, she thinks, running her tongue over her lower lip. *Kiss me. Grab my hair and kiss me!*

"You're different with him," Adam says softly. "You're smaller. Quieter. You hold yourself back." His eyes burn into her. "Even your voice changes." He shakes his head and Natasha stares at him, wondering if it's disgust she sees painted across his face. "Do you love him?" he asks finally.

"What?" But Natasha heard him perfectly.

"Do you love him?"

"Of course I love him." She bristles, pulling back.

"That's what I thought." He stands, reaching out his hand and she stares at it, like it's a trick, a deception, like he's offering more than just a hand, but finally, she slips her hand into his, letting him pull her to her feet.

They stand on the sidewalk, only a foot separating them, breathing heavily, staring each other in the eyes. The world, once so stable, seems to spin. The earth tilting on its axis.

This is the moment.

This is what she's hoped for, wanting and dreading in equal measure.

He reaches up, brushing a lock of hair behind her ear, the gesture at once tender and devastating. She leans into his hand knowing everything she wants in that moment is written so clearly across her face.

His lips twitch and his hand falls to his side. And then he smiles, a tight little smile that feels like a slap. "Come on, it's late."

She follows after him, trailing behind, the moment on the sidewalk etched into her, the humiliation of knowing that he saw her desire so clearly painted on her face. That he knows that she wants him and simply turned away.

When they arrive at her building, she stares up at it, at the darkened windows, knowing that upstairs, Christopher is asleep in their bed and that in a few minutes, she'll be there next to him.

She walks towards the door, not stopping to say goodbye and Adam grabs her wrist, pulling her back.

She stares at him before shaking him off and his eyes, in the light of the marquis over her door, shine bright and cold.

"Adam," she says softly, shaking her head. Whatever might have happened has passed and she wants nothing more than the warmth of her bed, the acceptance of Christopher's arms after Adam's silent rebuff.

"Give me your number."

"What?"

"I want you to text me when you're safe and sound in your apartment."

"Don't be ridiculous."

The stern look he gives her answers her question. With an exasperated sigh, she rattles off her number and then heads for the door, letting it slam shut behind her and as she waits for the elevator, she can't help herself and chances one last look over her shoulder.

Adam stands outside where she left him, bathed in a warm yellow light against the dark night, his hands shoved in his pockets, watching her.

The elevator pings and the doors open and she steps inside, leaving Adam alone on the street.

CHAPTER SIXTEEN

"Do you know what happens to naughty little cock teases?"

Her eyes dart between his face and the belt held doubled over in his hand. She takes a step back nervously.

"Say it."

"They get punished." Her voice quivers. He's never used the belt before and the thought fills her with terror.

"That's right. And doll, you've definitely earned your punishment after last night."

Last night. She blanches. She thought she'd gotten away with her deception, but the look in her student's eyes tells a different story. He let her get away, she realizes, let her believe she'd won just to sweeten this moment.

He grasps her chin roughly, forcing her to meet his eyes. There, she catches a glimpse of the devil. For only a devil could derive such satisfaction from cruelty.

"I told you I owned you." Fingers press into her jaw until her lips part involuntarily. "What time does your husband come home?"

She does not lie. Cannot lie. "Eleven."

He laughs, releasing her face and she stumbles back. "That gives us plenty of time." His eyes, dark as night, burn her skin as he takes her in. "Strip."

After last night, she knows any protest would be in vain, insufficient in the face of the inevitable.

His smug satisfaction when she complies without protest is worse than any physical torment.

She cannot deny any longer the truth.

He owns her.

Naked before her student in her marital bedroom, she is overcome with shame. It burns her, incandescent, a funeral pyre to her former self.

It isn't until he runs one finger over her bare cunt that she realizes the humiliating truth. Despite her protests. Despite her insistence that she does not want this, she is sopping wet.

He laughs at her mortification. "Suck." He shoves his finger past her lips and he watches, satisfied, as she sucks him hard.

"Get on the bed. Knees and forearms." When she hesitates, he cracks the belt on his open palm. "Now!"

She scrambles to obey, but she has to try one final time. "Please, he'll see! Anything but this. Please!"

"You should have thought about that before you disobeyed me." He runs the cool leather over her exposed backside making her flinch. "And Natalia, when I'm done with you, when your greedy cunt is filled with my seed, you will thank me. And when he comes home, drunk and horny after a night flirting with cocktail waitresses, and my seed is spilling from your cunt, I expect you to please him just as you would please me."

She shakes, shame and arousal leaving her dizzy.

"You're my whore. And that's what good little whores do. They obey their masters."

Natasha reaches for phone, still anticipating the first

deafening crack of the imaginary belt and red welt left in its wake.

What are you wearing?

Laughter bubbles out of her throat. Adam. And she wonders, staring at the screen, if this is the real reason he asked for her phone number.

Not the most original line I've ever heard, she texts back.

Humor me.

She imagines the impatient twitch of Adam's strong jaw, the way his eyebrows draw together.

After the things he's said to her, the thought of making him suffer, just a little, makes her grin.

Transparent white silk dress. Garter. Seamed stockings. Very high heels.

She holds her breath and waits. Thankfully, he doesn't make her wait long.

Panties?

No.

That's my girl. Where are you?

My office. Off-campus.

Are you alone?

Yes.

Good. Do something for me.

A shiver runs down her spine and he must take her silence for acquiescence because a second later, her phone beeps.

Touch yourself.

With pleasure.

Blood pounds in her ears as she slides one hand up her thigh, letting her legs fall open. The silk beneath her fingers is cool and smooth and when she reaches the top of her stockings, her bare flesh quivers as goose bumps

119

appear.

Are you wet?

Her fingers dance higher, toying with her sex, her slick moisture hot as she rubs her throbbing clit.

Yes.

Slide a finger inside your pussy for me.

For me. Eyes closed, she does, letting her legs fall wider as she imagines Adam kneeling between them, fucking her with his long fingers. She debates touching her nipples, twisting them until she feels that electric current running between nipple and cunt. Instead, she waits for Adam's next command as she leisurely moves her finger, one tantalizing finger, in and out, in and out, slow, teasing, setting her skin on fire. Without touching her clit, she won't come. She'll hover indefinitely at the edge, hips rocking, each minute movement magnified, amplified, deafening.

She stares at her phone, willing it to ring.

Finally, when it does, she feels her heart rate accelerate. Excitement courses through her.

Taste yourself. Taste yourself because I want to taste you. Let me taste you.

She moans, parting her lips to lick her musky arousal from her fingers. *I taste amazing.*

I know you do. I want to spend an entire night between your thighs, my tongue on your clit, my fingers massaging your g-spot. I want to watch you come over and over again.

Are you hard?

Hard doesn't begin to describe it. All I can think about is your mouth on my cock as you play with yourself, as you get yourself off.

She shivers. With wet fingers, she rolls her nipples until she moans, a low groan torn from the base of her throat.

Are you close?

Yes.

Come for me.

Yes.

Her fingers pick up speed, pleasure spiraling, spinning, her head thrown back, hips rolling, body pulsing, lust crashing like brutal waves over her.

Her orgasm, hot, fast, convulsive, yanks her from reality.

Panting, mouth parched, head spinning, body slowly floating down to earth, mind slowly returning.

Did you come?

Yes.

Good.

She stares at the phone in breathless wonder, wanting more, until finally, she leans back and laughs.

She expects to feel guilty when she comes home to Christopher, sitting on the couch in the living room, his reading glasses slipping low on his nose as he read.

Instead, she feels only desire, the slow simmering desire she has felt since Adam texted her earlier. The desire that cannot be quenched with merely an orgasm.

Christopher smiles at her, beckoning her with one crooked finger. "Give me a kiss."

"No." She shakes her hair loose as she unbuttons her shirt, pulling it out of her tight teal pencil skirt, keeping her eyes locked on his. He sits up, putting his book aside and takes off his reading glasses, folding them carefully before placing them on the armrest.

"No?" His blue eyes sparkle with amusement.

"No." Tossing aside her shirt, she shimmies out of her

skirt. And when she begins stroking her pussy, still wet from earlier, a flash of arousal crosses Christopher's face. With a knowing smile, she places one foot on the couch, bending her knee so her pussy is on full display as she buries two fingers inside. The scent of her arousal fills the air, reminding her of summer, green houses, the tropics. A rich, earthy smell like damp soil.

She lets her eyes traverse his body, smiling as she notices the bulge in his pants, his erection begging to be released as it pulls against his zipper.

"Natasha..." He reaches for her, his expression needy with lust, but she only shakes her head, pulling back.

"Not yet."

He stares at her, mystified, this stranger, this woman he thought he knew. She watches as he debates what to do, as he struggles to understand the game they are playing and finally, he pulls back, watching her as he slowly, carefully, lowers his zipper as if waiting for her approval or disapproval.

The power is intoxicating. The sight of his erection, hard, pulsing with need, beaded with pre-cum, makes her mouth water. She watches him take it in his hand, stroking it firmly.

His expression makes her breath catch as a blush spreads across her chest.

"Do you want to fuck me, Christopher?" Her voice sounds strange, husky, unrecognizable.

"More than anything."

"How? How do you want to fuck me?" She leans forward, eyes wide, her smile cruel as she pumps her fingers in and out of her pussy, waiting for his response. She wants to hear him say it. Wants to detail every naughty, delicious thing he wants to do to her before she lets him.

With a smile that makes her heart race, he shakes his head. "I want you to sit on my lap and take everything you want from me."

A quick stab of disappointment. And then she smiles. "Lick me first."

Christopher enthusiastically scoots forward, gripping her hips with his hand and pulling her towards his mouth.

"With pleasure."

Natasha moans as his tongue flicks across her open sex, her head falling back as he licks her expertly.

CHAPTER SEVENTEEN

Natasha stands confidently at the front of the room, a wry smile on her face knowing that beneath the burnt orange pencil skirt, she's not wearing panties. As her students file in, noisy, animated, her excitement peaks.

Adam.

She shifts, crossing her arms over her chest, waiting. Excitement is a drug, arousal a stimulant, spurring her on, making her decisions rash and unpredictable and utterly exhilarating.

Like a long walk on a brisk, fall afternoon.

The thumping of her heart reminds her that she is alive, that her future has not yet been determined.

But as the minutes tick by and Adam doesn't appear, her excitement turns to nervous agitation. Adam is never late and he's late now.

Christopher never made her feel this way. This unsteady. This uncertain. All Adam has to do is say one sexy word and she feels high. One harsh word, and she feels crushed beneath some unspeakable weight.

Christopher, from the very beginning, made his intentions clear. He wanted her. Wanted to love her. Wanted to make love to her. Wanted more than just sex.

And Natasha, so accustomed to his constant love, had forgotten what it felt like to be this unstable.

With one final glance at the clock, she forces herself to begin, though she wants, more than anything, to wait for him. "What do you think of when you think of plot?"

Colin raises his hand. "The action of the story."

"And is plot necessary?"

Her students look around, suspecting it's a trick question. Not one hand goes up. When the door opens, Natasha refuses to look, to confirm with her eyes what she knows from the frantic beat of her heart.

Adam.

Most students slink into class when they are late, but Adam enters proudly, without apology, dropping a folded piece of paper on her desk before taking his usual seat in the front row.

His lips move. *Sorry.*

She glances at her watch, frowning, irritated by both the disruption and also her response to his presence. "In the future, if you're more than ten minutes late, don't bother showing up."

She'll treat him like any other student. No special treatment. No easy outs.

"As I was saying. Can you have a story without plot?"

When no one responds, she sighs theatrically. "Come on, guys. Think." She expects Adam to say something and when he doesn't, she takes out a copy of their reading assignment, a Hemingway story she's loved since the first time she read it years before. "Okay, what is the plot of

"Hills like White Elephants"?"

"A woman's abortion?"

She raises one eyebrow. "Is that the plot or is that what the story is about?"

By the time they get to the workshop portion of the class, Adam is his usual self. Whatever has passed between them left outside the doors to the classroom and while she's thankful for this, Natasha can't help but wonder. It all felt so real, so potent, and now, she wonders if it wasn't just a dream.

Adam gives nothing away.

Class lets out and he gives her a smile before disappearing into the hall.

Natasha leans back, closing her eyes, feeling the world beneath her spin. It was all too real to have been invented. Too real.

With a deep breath, she begins collecting her things, only then seeing the folded piece of paper Adam dropped on her desk when he came in. She carefully unfolds it and when she reads it, she can't hide her smile.

Dear Professor Carson –

Please excuse Adam LaRue for his tardiness. He's suffered uncontrollable hard-ons since last night and had to stop in the restroom to relieve himself so he wouldn't spend the entire class fantasizing about bending you over the desk and fucking you. Hard.

Hard is underlined twice.

Natasha, laughing, slips the note into her wallet for safekeeping. She heads to the library, knowing that she has to prepare for classes. She's been so lost in everything, she has barely been able to focus.

Natasha is sitting in the main reading room of the central library on campus, surrounded by students staring into laptop screens, preparing for class, when Adam texts her.

If I whipped your skirt up and spanked you, how turned on would you be?

Unbelievably turned on. She bites her lip. Every time she responds to one of his messages, she feels a needling panic. What if he doesn't respond? What if all he wants is confirmation, proof that he can have her, proof that she's attracted to him and once he has it, once he knows she wants to play, he'll walk away, the game no longer interesting.

How hard am I spanking you?

She sighs with relief. *You start light. End hard.*

Am I spanking just your ass or making some contact with your pussy?

Just my ass. But in between strikes, you touch my pussy. You tease my clit.

Did you do something to deserve being punished or am I doing this just because I can?

Both. You don't need a reason to punish me but you find one anyway.

Her nipples bead against the material of her bra, her pussy clenches in frustration. All around her, students work, too busy to notice. She's thankful for the anonymity of a crowded room. She knows she's blushing. She can barely stop grinning. But not one person looks at her.

Discreetly, she passes her hand over her breast, pretending to brush something off her sweater, the contact electric and unsatisfying. Would anyone notice if she touched herself? Would anyone really look up from their computer screens long enough to realize what she's doing?

Does she really care?

Her face burns.

I spank you because I can and because it turns me on watching you squirm. Feeling your struggling body against my cock. I tell you it's because you've been naughty but we both know that's bullshit. I do it because it makes me hard and that's the only reason I need.

Between her legs, desire blossoms. She debates packing up her things, finding somewhere private, a bathroom or a deserted corner of the stacks where she can be alone, where she can touch herself without being seen, the possibility of being caught adding to the thrill.

Instead, she remains seated, enjoying the juxtaposition of her tame surroundings with Adam's lewd messages.

How hard?

Hard enough that I'm afraid I'll come if you don't stop moving.

She feels hot, playful, irreverent as she texts back. *Make me.*

She imagines a low growl, feral, an animal about to pounce. Adam, wild, unleashed, no longer pretending to be civilized.

Fuck civilized. She's had enough civilized to last her a lifetime. No, what she wants is rough. Primal. Raw. Desire and lust unleashed, without restraint or inhibition.

The cursor blinks and she licks her lips. Adam, typing. *Where are you?*

Her fingers shake. *The library.*

The blinking cursor. Her heart in her throat as she waits.

"Sending raunchy texts to Christopher again?"

Natasha jumps, her heart leaping in her chest. With a roll of her eyes, Maggie dumps her heavy purse on the table between them and slumps into the once vacant chair across from Natasha.

Natasha grabs her phone, concealing it in her lap.

What the hell has she been thinking? When her phone vibrates, she ignores it. This can't go on. She has to stop. Because Adam makes her want to do things that she shouldn't do.

Was she really thinking of touching herself here, in the library, at the university where she teaches?

But one look at Maggie's face, crumpled up like a wet paper towel, sends all thoughts of Adam out of her mind. "What's wrong?"

Maggie looks up from studying her hands, her green eyes widening as her forehead wrinkles. "That son of a bitch called again. He's coming into town for a week."

Natasha doesn't have to ask who "that son of a bitch" is. Marco. She's never met him but she's seen pictures. Gorgeous Marco. A blue eyed, dark haired devil of a man with no regard for the way his sudden appearances and just as sudden disappearances wreak havoc on the woman he still, after a bottle of wine, claims to love.

He may look like an underwear model, but he's always reminded Natasha of a cockroach, appearing after dark then scuttling off at the first sign of light.

"No. Tell him no. He can't keep doing this."

"I know, I know," Maggie says, smiling weakly. "It's stupid and self-destructive but I can't say no."

Natasha has no leg to stand on, but she's seen firsthand the way Marco's appearances destroy Maggie, the guilt and the self-doubt that always follow his return home. And no matter how many times Maggie declares enough is enough, she keeps letting him back in.

Natasha sighs. "Remember being twenty-two and thinking we'd hit thirty and suddenly have everything figured out?"

Maggie laughs. "God, we were such idiots."

"When's he getting in?"

"Thursday." She makes a face. "If he even shows. God, why do I keep doing this to myself?"

"Because he's disgustingly good-looking."

"It really is disgusting, isn't it? Plus, he's stunning in the sack. Who would have guessed such an insufferable narcissist could be such a gifted lover?"

"It's really unbelievable."

"I'm sure he gets off on the idea of being the best lover on earth, so really, it's still all about him."

"Will you keep your voices down? Some of us are actually trying to work," a student at a nearby table says in a low, angry voice, glaring in their direction.

Natasha glares right back. "Come on, let's grab a drink before I have to go home."

"Christopher keeping you on a tight leash?"

Natasha shrugs and begins dumping her things into her tote bag. The last thing she wants to think about right now is Christopher.

They push open the heavy front doors of the library, stepping into the crisp fall evening.

"Professor Carson."

Natasha stumbles at the sound of Adam's husky voice, and he rushes towards her, placing one hand on her low back to steady her.

Natasha pulls away, straightening stiffly.

"Adam, right?"

Adam smiles at Maggie. "Professor Green."

"I think after I've killed you in darts you could at least call me Maggie," she says, her face lighting up.

"It's good to see you again, Maggie."

"We're off to get a drink. Come. Keep us company. I need a distraction and you look very distracting."

His low laughter rumbles through Natasha's chest and she opens her mouth about to protest, but he beats her to it.

"I'd love to."

CHAPTER EIGHTEEN

From their table on the roof terrace of The Summit, they watch the sun dip behind the apartment buildings on Riverside Drive, turning the windows gold in the last dying light of the day. The air is cool but the sky is clear. Natasha hugs her sweater around her shoulders, an unnecessary gesture under the warmth of the heat lamps.

"You're one of the fellows, right?" Maggie asks, sipping her beer. "Does that mean you'll be teaching here in the fall?"

Adam shrugs his broad shoulders. "I guess that depends on whether or not anyone wants me here," he responds slowly. "I want to keep my options open. A lot could change between now and September."

"Do you even want to teach?" Natasha asks, her question coming out more hostile than she intends, but the idea of Adam remaining here, on campus, after he graduates makes her antsy.

"Poetry isn't going to pay the bills." His curious expression makes Natasha regret asking. "What do you think? Is it worth it? Giving up the time and the freedom?"

"Depends on the person, I guess," she answers noncommittally, wondering if it's really teaching he's talking about.

He holds her gaze for a moment longer than necessary before turning to Maggie. "What do you think?"

She grins. "I love it."

"You don't want to write full-time?"

"God no!" Maggie laughs. "Tried it. Hated it. I'm pathologically afraid of being alone. Lord knows why I became a writer."

"Yeah, that seems problematic."

"I've figured out enough tricks to get around it."

"Writing groups," Natasha adds. "And hair dressers."

"Hair dressers?" Adam lifts one eyebrow. "I'll bite. What do hair dressers have to do with anything?"

Maggie brushes her tight curls out of her face. "Once a month, I get my hair done at a salon. You know how they massage your scalp? It's the best." She shrugs, but she's smiling, not the slightest bit embarrassed. "Hair dressers are like prostitutes. Or masseuses. They keep me sane."

Adam swivels his head towards Natasha. "I should be taking notes, shouldn't I? The truth about writers. What about you? Any quirky tricks for maintaining sanity?" His voice is playful, teasing.

Natasha thinks of her pleasure chest, her studio apartment without internet, the sexual games she plays with herself, but shakes her head. "I like being alone."

"That's because you're never alone," Maggie quips.

Natasha's temple pulses, the first sign of an impending migraine. Alcohol will only make it worse, but she takes a sip of her beer anyway, hating the truth behind Maggie's off-handed remark. When was she last single? When was the last time she slept more than a few nights in a bed by herself?

Thankfully, Adam changes the topic. "I'm supposed to be distracting you, but I can't properly do my job if I don't know what I'm up against."

"He who shall not be named," Maggie says, rolling her eyes.

"Ex or family member?"

"Ex. Though at a certain point, the line between the two seems purely theoretical."

"What did he do?" Adam leans forward, planting his elbows on the table as he searches Maggie's face. "Am I going to have to break some kneecaps? I'm not a naturally violent man but exceptions can be made."

Maggie laughs and for the first time since showing up in the library, she looks like her usual self, not the least bit worried about Marco. "If only." She pushes her chair back. "Sadly, I think he'd find having his kneecaps broken further sign of his unspeakable sex appeal." She shakes her head, and Natasha can see the affection in that gesture, the love she still holds for Marco, in spite of everything. "Off to the ladies' and I expect a fresh pitcher of beer on the table when I return."

The moment Maggie disappears from sight, Natasha shifts her attention to Adam. Watching Maggie with him, the easy banter and the way her face lights up, Natasha knows that she is being selfish.

"You're attracted to her."

"She's an attractive woman," he says slowly.

"She is." Natasha takes a deep breath. "But are you attracted to her?"

His eyes narrow. "I'm not trying to sleep with her, if that's what you're asking."

She shakes her head, thinking about the look on Maggie's face right before she got up. "I want you to sleep with her."

"You've got to be fucking kidding."

"You've never seen her after he leaves."

He leans back, carefully studying her. "Is that what you really want?" His voice, low and dangerous, makes her flinch.

"Yes."

He turns away from her and flags down the cocktail waitress to order another pitcher of beer just as Maggie returns from the bathroom.

"Let's see if we can't get you to forget all about the man whose name shall not be uttered," Adam says, pointedly ignoring Natasha as he lifts his glass to Maggie, who smiles, brushing back her hair and clinks glasses with him.

"Cheers."

Adam doesn't look at Natasha. He doesn't toast her. Instead, he focuses his attention entirely on Maggie, his body angled towards her, his hands, resting on the table, mere inches from Maggie's.

It feels like someone is cutting her chest open with a knife, but Natasha can't look away. She asked him to do this. This is what she wants. For Maggie to forget Marco. For Maggie to remember there are men out there, gorgeous men, who can be sweet and kind and who don't disappear the moment they've snaked their way back into your bed.

For Adam to remind her that there are men out there

worthy of her time.

But all of her good intentions don't make it any easier to watch.

She drains her beer before pushing back her chair, flinching as the metal scrapes against the poured concrete floor. "I should go."

Adam lifts one eyebrow and she can see the challenge in his eyes, the dare, but Natasha can't stay. She can't watch.

"Are you sure? Stay for fifteen minutes and we can leave together," Maggie suggests.

"No, don't be silly. Stay. Have fun." She forces herself to smile as she drops a twenty onto the table, but the moment she's out of view, the smile drops away and as she hurries towards home, all she can think is that the pain in the center of her chest, that acute physical pain, is all of her own doing.

When Christopher comes home, Natasha's in bed, the lights out, the blankets pulled up around her neck. She listens to him puttering about the apartment as she pretends to sleep. And when he finally gets into bed, reaching his large, beautiful hands beneath her shirt, feeling her skin hot with fever, she rolls over, away from him.

For the first time in her life, Natasha Carson has no interest in sex.

CHAPTER NINETEEN

Natasha spends the entire morning checking her phone with a sick feeling at the pit of her stomach, hoping for some word from Maggie. Some confirmation that Adam did what she asked him. Nothing. In that deafening silence, she hears all the confirmation she needs. She hears Maggie telling her, in excruciating detail, what a marvelous lover he is. How he lavished her body with attention, leaving no part untouched, no part unexplored. How she woke up, sated and dying for more.

Christopher asks if she's feeling okay, and she jumps, too agitated to pretend everything is fine.

"It's nothing important," she lies, seeing the concern in his eyes, but he doesn't push and she's thankful for that at least.

She's half expecting Adam not to show up, too busy locked in a passionate embrace with Maggie to remember something as meaningless as class. Her class.

But he's there, on time, looking the same as always. Perfectly cool without the least bit of effort. When he isn't looking, she scrutinizes his appearance, searching for something. Some sign. Some indication of where he spent the night.

But there's nothing. Nothing to tell her if he slept alone or not.

At least he's changed. He's wearing the same black jeans he wears most days, but today, he's dressed in a wrinkled pale blue shirt that looks like something he pulled off the floor in a hurry and Natasha hates herself for noticing, hates herself for feeling this undone when she has no right. She has no right to Adam. No right at all. How can she be angry with him for doing something she asked him to do? Practically begged him to do.

Was it masochism that made her do it? A need to hurt? Or worse, did she ask him as a test?

The two-hour class drags by. Her smile feels brittle. And she is afraid, if someone says the wrong word, she'll crack under the strain.

As she's packing up her things, Adam approaches her desk. The other students are leaving, discussing plans for the night, but all she can feel is Adam's lingering presence, so close and yet, not quite close enough.

"Are you mad at me?"

She brushes her hair out of her eyes and squints at him. "Of course not."

"Funny, because you haven't looked me in the eye once."

She glares at him. "Happy?"

He shakes his head. "No."

She looks away and angrily shoves the last of her things into her bag. "You should go."

"No."

She yanks her bag off the table, hoisting it over her shoulder. "Fine." She only takes three steps when Adam grabs her arm, spinning her around forcefully.

His expression is unreadable, but she can detect the current of tension below the surface. "We need to talk."

"There's nothing to talk about."

"Bullshit."

She pulls her arm free. "Did you have fun last night?"

The moment the words leave her mouth, Natasha regrets them. She has no right to be angry. No right.

His lips twitch as he tries to suppress a smile. "I did," he says slowly and Natasha flinches. "Would you like to hear what happened after you left? Every sordid detail? Every little touch and caress and promise?" He stares her down and she steps back, almost expecting him to stop her, but he doesn't. The muscles in his jaw jump and she can't tell what emotion lurks beneath that stare, only that it makes her nervous, only that he sounds angry.

"You don't owe me any explanation," she backtracks quickly.

"That's where you're wrong." He takes a step towards her, crowding her and she is once again aware of his towering height, his muscular body and also his scent, that glorious scent of his. She shakes her head but she doesn't know what she's even denying. Her mind is running in circles, too fast for her to keep up.

"I – I have to go," she says at last.

"We aren't done."

"Yes. We are." She pushes past him and walks out the door, holding her head up, trying to maintain whatever small shred of dignity she has left.

If there's anything left to salvage.

The door slams shut behind her and she finds herself hoping that he'll follow after her, that he'll chase her down.

When he doesn't, the disappointment is almost enough to knock her off her feet.

CHAPTER TWENTY

"I own you. Not the other way around."

She's tied to a chair, her legs spread open and secured with rope. The room is suffocating, the heat making her light-headed. She wants to beg him to change his mind, but she knows from experience that begging has no effect on him. He is hard. Uncompromising. And once his mind is made up, there is no changing it.

His expression is cruel, sinister as he approaches her, trailing his hand over her shoulder, down her side then up again to cup her breast. She leans into his hand, hating herself. He pinches her nipple, twisting it cruelly but she bites her lip, her only protest to deprive him of the satisfaction of hearing her pain.

He smiles, removing a vibrator from his pocket. And when he slips it between the lips of her pussy, she tries to arch her hips but she is too tightly bound.

"Enjoy the show," he says, laughing as he walks away without turning on the vibrator. He leaves the room and Natalia drops her head to her chest in defeat.

Minutes or hours pass. When Alex returns, he's followed by a woman who is both beautiful and naked. The look he gives her makes her blood go cold.

There's a bed in the center of the room where Alex has taken her so many times, where he's defiled her, where she has begged for his cock even as her mind told her, again and again that it was wrong, that this was wrong, that everything he was doing was against her will.

Now, the beautiful girl spreads herself on that bed, her docile expression so at odds with the suffering she's experienced in this room.

Natalia expects him to tie her down. To beat her long and hard before allowing her the pleasure of his cock. The vibrator between her legs suddenly feels impossibly hard, painful, as it sits, inert, lodged inside of her.

Instead, Alex throws Natalia one final look over his shoulder, and she can see his power over her in that single gaze, before he focuses his attention on the woman laying before him so eagerly and so willingly.

With hands so gentle, he nudges her legs apart, bending them at the knees so that she is fully exposed to him. And then he begins to pleasure her. He is never forceful. Never the cruel beast he is with Natalia. He kisses and licks his way from her knees to her sex and back down again on the other side. He caresses her breasts. The woman moans, her pleasure increasing as Natalia's pain and torment build, until it is all that Natalia can think, all she can feel. A betrayal worse than anything she has experienced until now.

For Alex does not fuck this woman. No. He makes love to her, gentle and slow, coaxing the woman once to orgasm before he ever enters her. He is slow, gentle, each thrust measured, paced, designed with the woman's pleasure in mind.

Natalia cannot help but think back to the last time he'd had her on that bed, with her legs bound open and her mouth gagged. Some nights, he liked to hear her screams. Others, he deprived her even of that one final right.

The woman's moans of pleasure are lashes against Natalia's skin, more biting than a beating by the cane.

That night, he'd refused to let her come. He'd fucked her mouth and her anus, not once coming in contact with her pussy, a torture designed to both humiliate and arouse her.

It had worked.

She'd left with makeup running down her face and her sex still on fire and his cum smeared across her ass.

As horrible as it sounds, Natalia yearns for that moment again. For anything, even denial, is better than this. Better than being forced to see the way he treats other women.

His words echo in her mind. I own you. Not the other way around.

Something inside of her breaks.

Natasha drops her face into her hands and lets out a long, strangled sigh. Writing was supposed to distract her, was supposed to keep her mind off Adam.

She doesn't own him. She has no right to him. No claim. Nothing at all. This isn't a schoolyard disagreement between friends. There can be no, "I saw him first."

She has Christopher.

She should be happy.

Still no word from Maggie. She debates texting her, casually asking about last night, but every time she picks up the phone, she can't bring herself to do it. She doesn't want to know. Maggie has never been one to keep the details of her private life private and Natasha doesn't think she can handle listening to a play by play of a night with Adam LaRue.

And doesn't she already know? Hasn't he given her

enough of an idea from the text messages, the brief conversations, the comments? Sex with Adam would be electric. Dangerous.

She wants to scream. Wants to throw something, watch something break, shatter, that satisfying sound of something coming apart, knowing that she was the one to break it. Instead, she goes to the kitchen and pours herself a glass of wine. She's been drinking too much lately. She blames Adam, but that's not fair. It isn't his fault that he makes her feel so undone. Like she's being held together by Scotch tape and blind will.

She downs the entire glass standing in the kitchen, her heart racing, and pours another. She should go home. She should go home, eat dinner with Christopher, make love to Christopher, take a long bath and go to sleep. Tomorrow is another day. Tomorrow everything that feels so overwhelming now, in this very moment, will seem foolish, trivial, meaningless.

Except Natasha can't make herself believe it. She picks up her phone and begins re-reading her texts with Adam. This brings her no comfort. But Natasha has always been the type of woman who enjoys picking a scab until it bleeds.

She dreads going home, dreads Christopher's unconditional love. The tender look in his eyes when he gazes at her. It makes her feel like a monster.

And yet, she can't turn away from him. When she sees him, she selfishly wraps her arms around him, holding on for dear life as she presses her lips to his chest, stealing the comfort of his embrace and hating herself for it.

For this weakness.

He kisses the crown of her head. It makes her feel like a child. It makes her feel safe.

"Mom called," he says, releasing her.

"And?" She's never been able to shake the feeling that his mother disapproves of her somehow. Of course, she's never been anything but polite to her, but still, that feeling, of silent disapproval lingers in the air like an accusation. What are you doing with my son? How are you using him? You're too young. You're not good enough.

"She wants to make sure we're still coming for Thanksgiving."

"That's a million years from now."

"You know mom." He shrugs. "If she doesn't know who's bringing the pumpkin pie at least six weeks in advance, she panics."

Natasha swallows painfully. "Of course we'll be there."

A tiny voice in her head asks if that's a promise she can really make.

"Great." Christopher kisses her cheek and she forces herself to smile. "I'll let her know. You know how happy it makes her that we spend Thanksgiving up there."

Her phone ringing in the other room is a welcome distraction and she kisses Christopher one last time before setting off to get it, both hoping and dreading it will be Maggie.

It's not.

Adam's name flashes on the screen.

She almost sends it to voicemail, but at the last minute, she answers, walking down the hallway towards their bedroom, away from Christopher. "What?"

"I told you we aren't finished talking."

"I can't do this right now," she says impatiently.

Talking about Thanksgiving makes her anxious.

"Is Christopher there?"

"Yes."

"Then don't talk. Listen."

She plops down on the bed, slipping her feet from her shoes and cradling her phone against her neck. She rubs her feet, sore after a day squeezed into heels. She loves heels, loves the way they make her look and feel, but at the end of the day, they really are just another form of torture.

"You can deny it all you want. You can tell me you don't want me. Hell, you can tell yourself that you don't want me, but we both know that's bullshit. I don't know if you're happy with Christopher. I don't know if he is everything you've ever wanted. But I know, when you look at me, I feel alive. And I can see it in your face. You feel it too."

Natasha falls back, letting her head hit the pillows and holds her breath.

"Do you have any idea how many times I've come thinking about you? The first time I read *Forced Seduction*--" He laughs. "- I thought, is it possible to fall in love with someone you've never met? Because I thought I loved you. Layla Allen. This fearless, badass woman who didn't give a fuck what anyone thought. She just did what she wanted and spat in the face of anyone who thought what she was doing was wrong. I must have put that book down a hundred times so I could jack off, just thinking about this fantasy woman I knew I'd never get to meet."

Adam's voice is husky and melodic and it's easy for Natasha to close her eyes and let it swirl around her, let it transport her to another place.

"And then I read *Hunger* and something clicked. I just

knew. It had to be you. You had to be Layla. I watched you for an entire semester before I asked to take your class. An entire semester. I watched you wander campus with a glazed look in your eyes, like you were somewhere else. I watched you with *him*. You were nothing like how I imagined. I imagined leather and chains and a loud, brash voice that sent people scurrying. Instead, you smiled politely. You yielded.

"But I still wanted you. Hell, I wanted you even more, knowing that you lead this perfect double life. Half the time you were prim and proper and the rest of the time, you were whipping imaginary girls in dank basements so people like me could get off. And let me tell you, I did."

Natasha's breath catches and she feels the slow creep of arousal listening to Adam.

"I kept thinking, maybe I'm wrong. Maybe I got all the signs mixed up. Hell, for a while there, I thought Layla Allen might have been a name Christopher used. But it didn't make sense. The only thing that made sense was you. In those insane pencil skirts of yours and your high heels. You have no idea how hard it was for me to reconcile the two images. Do you want to know the moment I finally knew I was right?"

Natasha swallows the lump in her throat. "Yes." Her voice cracks.

"Last year's thesis party. You were wearing that red dress and seamed stockings and you were standing alone in a corner. You looked like there wasn't a place in the world you'd rather be less than that auditorium. And then you got this funny look in your eyes. You scribbled something on a napkin and I could see all the gears turning in your head, all the synapses firing at once, that perfect synchronicity when you solve some problem you've been working over in your head. You kept biting your lip. And then you smiled. This radiant smile that wasn't for anyone but you, but I told myself you were smiling for me. And then, just like that, I watched you crumple the napkin you were writing on in your hand and toss it into the trash can. I went through the trash and found the napkin. Do you know what it said?"

Natasha remembers that night perfectly. It was a terrible night. She didn't want to go, but Christopher insisted, it was their job and she knew he was right even though she hated him for it. She was writing a book called *The Servant Girl* and it was almost done, the only thing she couldn't figure out was a perfect title. It's funny, she can write a book in a month, but it takes her just as long to come up with the three words that eventually grace the cover.

"*Blackest Desire*," she whispers. That was the name that came to her as she ignored the room full of people that night.

"Why throw it away?"

"I knew I wouldn't forget." After she threw the cocktail napkin in the trash, she'd gone in search of Christopher, never looking back. If she had, would she have noticed Adam leaning over the trashcan?

After Christopher fell asleep that night, she snuck into the living room and put the finishing touches on the book.

"That's how I knew I wasn't crazy. When you published *Blackest Desire*, I felt like I'd somehow been a part of it. Of course, I knew I wasn't. But I was there when you came up with it, I was watching you when you thought of it, and somehow, I told myself I was the reason. I was the inspiration."

She says nothing. She closes her eyes and thinks about that night. How could she have missed Adam? How is it possible she never noticed him until he set foot in her classroom? He's too good looking to blend into the scenery, too intense to dissolve into the background, and yet, for an entire year, they orbited one another without her knowledge.

It makes her inexplicitly sad.

"I read *Blackest Desire* and I said to myself, this is the woman I have to be with. Even if it's just one night. Natasha, you are inside me. I close my eyes at night and hear your voice. It doesn't matter who I fuck, that feeling, that ache never goes away. I'm hard now, knowing you're on the other end of the line. That you're listening to me. You don't have to say anything. You don't have to do anything. Just listen. Listen to what you do to me."

As he spoke, Adam's voice grew huskier and Natasha swallows hard, knowing that he is aroused and that his arousal is making her body heat up.

"Oh god, Natasha," he growls, and she knows he has his dick in his hand, that he's masturbating and it makes her wet. "Every time I come, I come thinking about you," he sighs. "I think about you all the time. I think about fucking you. About sinking my cock into you, feeling your wet hot heat squeezing me. I doubt I'd last five minutes inside of you the first time. I wouldn't be able to help myself. But afterwards," he growls, emitting a low sound that makes Natasha's nipples tighten, "afterwards, I'd spend the entire night making it up to you. Anything and everything you wanted."

The sound of his heavy breathing. The sound of his

hand around his cock as he pleasures himself. Natasha yearns to slip her hand down her pants and stroke her clit to the rhythm of his breathing.

"I want to taste your pussy. I want to bury my face between your legs and feast until you melt. Until you scream my name."

She can almost smell it. Almost taste it. She bites her lip, a moan hovering at the back of her throat.

She opens her eyes and looks around the bedroom. She is still alone. Adam pants into the phone. She slips into the bathroom, locking the door behind her and letting the water run from the faucet.

"Don't stop." She sinks to the floor, her back pressed against the bathtub, her legs spread. She pushes her hand into her jeans, jumping when her fingers brush her clit.

"Are you touching yourself?"

She shivers. "Yes."

"Close your eyes."

She does, letting his voice carry her away. "Can you feel it? Can you feel how much I want you? How much I need you?"

She rubs her clit, moaning softly, letting him hear her. "Keep going," she begs.

"Every day, I fight the urge to bend you over the desk and yank up your skirt and fuck you right there, where anyone and everyone can see. And you'd let me. You'd beg me to fuck you harder, to slap your ass until you scream. Come for me. Let me hear you."

The raw desperation in his voice sends Natasha crashing over the edge, her orgasm shaking her violently, her muscles clenching, her body rippling. "Adam," she moans.

With a roar, she hears him come. Shakily, she gets to her feet, her phone clutched in her damp fingers.

"Natasha."

"Yes?"

"When you fuck Christopher tonight, I want you to close your eyes and imagine I'm the one making you come."

With that, he disconnects and Natasha is left staring at her reflection in the bathroom mirror. Her cheeks are flushed and her heart is racing and she feels, for the first time in a very long while, completely and utterly alive.

CHAPTER TWENTY-ONE

"You are such an asshole," Maggie declares, bursting into Natasha's office, her cheeks flushed with excitement.

"What did I do this time?" But even as Natasha strives to keep her voice even and light, her mind races, trying to think of what she might have done and worse, how Maggie might have found out.

"Adam," Maggie says with a sigh, sinking into the chair across from her. "How could you leave me with him in a bar full of booze and fail to mention he has a girlfriend?"

Her stomach twists painfully. "What?" But luckily, Maggie is too distracted by her story to see her pained expression or the way she sits up unusually straight.

"There I was thinking, if ever there was a man who could fuck the memory of Marco out of me, this is that man. We have a few drinks. He's super flirty. He keeps putting his hand on my knee and I'm thinking, Mags, tonight you are finally breaking this dry spell. And then, you know what he says?" Maggie stares pointedly at her. "He says, 'Maggie, if I weren't involved with someone, I'd

155

take you home this second and fuck you until you hear the name Marco and say, who?'"

Natasha swallows the lump in her throat. "What happened?"

"Nothing. Abso-fucking-lutely nothing. We finished our drinks, paid and he hailed me a cab. And then, just as I'm about to get into the cab, he grabs my hand, kisses it, and says, 'There's a man out there who would move mountains to be with you. Why settle for someone who expects you to move the mountains instead?' That's it. I get home, hornier than hell, and spend the rest of the evening watching re-runs of *Gossip Girl* and masturbating. The end."

Maggie leans back, sipping her coffee as she watches Natasha.

"I feel like I'm missing something but I'm too tired to be thinking clearly," Natasha finally says.

"Nope. Nothing. Seriously." Another theatrically sigh as Maggie puts her legs up on Natasha's desk. "Tell me you know who he's dating so I can kill her, stash the body somewhere and claim him as mine."

Natasha laughs nervously, relief coursing through her when she realizes that Maggie has no idea about her and Adam. Not that there is a her and Adam. Only in her head. And on paper.

But her relief is short lived. What if he is dating someone? What if, while he's calling her and masturbating over the phone, there's a woman sitting in the next room, feet up, watching television, waiting for him to come back and take her out to dinner and fuck her senseless?

The thought makes her stomach knot up. Until this moment, she never considered the possibility that Adam isn't single. And the more she thinks about it, the less plausible it seems. He's gorgeous. He could have any woman he wanted. As her mind races, she prays that he only said it to make Maggie feel better, because the idea of him having a girlfriend makes her feel physically ill.

She forces herself to smile. "Sorry, no luck. I don't exactly grill students on their personal lives."

"You are a terrible friend." Maggie faux pouts.

"I know. The absolute worst."

With a groan, Maggie drops her feet back to the floor and pushes herself up. "Well, that's it. That's my story. I'm off."

"I thought we were having lunch."

"Nope. There's something I need to do."

"Please tell me it involves calling Marco and telling him to go fuck himself."

Maggie grins. "Marco who?"

Natasha spends the day repeating the mantra, I will not contact Adam, I will not contact Adam, I will not contact Adam, but by six o'clock, it's all she can think about, making it impossible to focus on anything else.

She hesitates, biting her lip as she stares at the phone, trying to find the best way to ask him without sounding like a jealous lunatic, even though, at this moment, that's exactly how she feels. Like a jealous lunatic. Finally, she works up the courage, screwing up her face nervously as she texts him one question. *Do you have a girlfriend?*

The second she hits send, she switches off her phone. She refuses to sit around anxiously worrying about what he'll say.

Instead, on the way home, she stops first at the grocery

store, picking up a rotisserie chicken, and then at the wine store for a nice bottle of pinot noir.

The first thing she does in the morning, after putting the coffee pot on, is turn on her phone and pace the kitchen, refusing to look at it.

The knot in her stomach has twisted tighter and her mouth is uncomfortably dry. She feels like an idiot, worried about what he will say, worried that he will tell her there's someone in his life more important than her when there is someone in her life more important than him.

The hypocrisy makes her want to vomit, but as she picks up her phone, she knows she has to look. That not knowing is worse than knowing, no matter what his answer.

She tells herself the reason she is so worried is she needs to know exactly what sort of mess she's stepped into. If he has a girlfriend, someone who might look at his phone and see their texts, it could ruin her. Universities don't exactly smile on professors who get involved with their students.

She's confident that Christopher would never check her phone, that there is no reason for her to erase the messages from Adam. He trusts her completely and his trust hurts almost as much as her infidelity. But if Adam has a girlfriend, all it would take is a single, irate phone call and Natasha would find herself out of a job.

Her phone chirps in quick succession, and she jumps, startled. There are six texts, all from Adam. She reads them in order and her hand, clutching the coffee mug for dear life, begins to tremble. She sets it down before she ends up spilling coffee all over the kitchen floor.

Jealous?

Five minutes later. *Will you please call me? This isn't a conversation I want to be having via text message.*

Two minutes later. *Goddamn it, pick up!*

Where are you?

Are you seriously ignoring me right now?

Ten minutes after that, the final text message. *No. I don't have a girlfriend. Will you please stop ignoring my calls. We have to talk.*

Natasha puts her phone down, screen facing the table, and stares at her hands. Whatever is going on between her and Adam, he isn't supposed to be angry. He doesn't have the right to make demands. That isn't the type of relationship they have.

She lets out a sigh of relief, her shoulders sagging. No girlfriend. No one to rat them out to the administration.

But she knows that isn't why she's relieved.

Fuck the administration. They could fire her and while the embarrassment would sting, it wouldn't be the end of the world.

No. The end of the world would be finding out that no matter what Adam said to her, no matter what he made her believe, he was in love with someone else.

Her fingers shake as she texts him back. *Sorry. Phone was off. I promise, I wasn't ignoring you. At least not intentionally.*

She doesn't expect a response. It's eight in the morning. But her phone chirps and the color drains from her face.

Meet me. Anywhere. I don't care. But I need to see you.

For a moment, she hesitates. Anywhere around campus is too risky. Whatever Adam thinks he has to say to her, she doesn't want it said anywhere near campus where someone might see them.

Chewing her lip, she texts him the address to her studio apartment.

I'll see you in an hour.

Christopher leaves, kissing her cheek and once he's out the door, she runs to the closet, trying to figure out what to wear. She doesn't want to look like she's trying. She wants to look casual and cool and like seeing him doesn't make her stomach tense with anxiety.

While teaching, she favors conservative dresses and pencil skirts because they make her feel the part. People are always telling her that she looks younger than her thirty years, and while she knows this is a compliment, it doesn't help establish her authority in the classroom.

This morning is different. And so she settles on black skinny jeans and a cozy sweater and then pulls her hair up into a messy bun.

Looking in the mirror, she's amazed by her appearance. Fresh faced. Youthful. She looks like a college student.

She barely recognizes herself.

She grabs her purse and leaves.

Adam is already there, waiting outside, smoking a cigarette, one hand tucked into the back pocket of his jeans, when she gets out of the taxi.

He doesn't move, but his eyes follow her, and the way he's looking at her does nothing to alleviate her nerves. Inviting him here was a mistake. It was definitely a mistake. But now that they are both here, there's no taking it back. No saying, Oops, why don't we go to the bodega for a cup of coffee instead even though I dragged you sixty blocks from home.

With a nervous smile, she digs her keys out of her bag, avoiding his eyes, and unlocks the front door.

CHAPTER TWENTY-TWO

The second the door to the apartment shuts, Adam grabs her, spinning her around and kissing her hard on the mouth. She stiffens, her lips parting in surprise. His tongue slips into her mouth, his kiss forceful, desperate and for a moment, Natasha forgets everything except the feel of him against her, his hard body, his kiss loosening whatever last hold on reality she has. She leans into him, her hands clutching for purchase as they devour each other in a fog of heat.

And then it hits her. Hard. Fast. She pushes against his chest, struggling to free herself because she knows that if she doesn't put a stop to this now, they won't be able to stop. *She* won't be able to stop.

With one final nip to her bottom lip, Adam steps back, panting and wipes his hand across his mouth.

"I couldn't resist." He grins, running one hand through his dark hair. Natasha takes another step back, needing to put distance between them, needing to put distance between her body and that kiss.

"Adam…" She trails off. Isn't this what she's wanted all along? She looks up at him, expecting to see some sign of guilt, some remorse, but she sees only desire as his eyes continue to rove over her body.

She realizes, suddenly, that this is the first time that they have been truly alone together.

He licks his lower lip and for a brief instant, Natasha imagines him coming at her. Grabbing her by the waist and pulling her to him. She sees his erection straining against his jeans.

Seeing Adam here, the first person to enter her studio since she rented it, she realizes that everything, from the bookshelves, to the haphazard art on the walls, was hung with her height in mind. He dwarves everything.

"What is this place?" he asks as he walks slowly towards the bed and trails the fingers of his right hand over the coverlet.

"My writing studio."

He glances over his shoulder, and Natasha knows she should look away. That looking at Adam is dangerous. He sees her. And that very act of seeing, of acceptance, threatens everything.

But Natasha doesn't look away. She can't.

"I've never brought anyone here before."

He raises one eyebrow and Natasha feels the weight of her admittance in his gaze. Carefully, he studies the small cluttered room, filled with her mementos, her writing fetish objects, her books. It's more than a room; it's the physical manifestation of her interior landscape.

His silence terrifies her.

"I like it," he says, turning away from the window and Natasha lets out a sigh of relief. With unhurried movements, he crosses the room. "It's perfect. Your apartment isn't you. It's too solid. Too conventional. Too neat and ordered. This," he sweeps his hand in front of him, "this is you."

She lets her eyes close and when she feels his thumb run softly across her full lower lip, bruised from his kiss, her mouth opens a fraction.

What is she doing? What is she thinking?

But the feeling, the subtlety of the gesture, makes such thoughts difficult, if not impossible. She hears the blood pounding in her ears. Anticipation is a drug, one best aged. The future, bright and filled with promise.

For all her sanctimonious proclamations, that she would never cheat, that she does not believe in cheating, she thinks back to Vermont. To the writing retreat. Those weeks in the lush mountains. Those weeks alone with Christopher. She has told the story so many times, she remembers not what happened, but the retelling. They went on walks. They shared work. They laughed. But is that all? Were there no stolen kisses? No lips brushing collarbones as they delved deeper into the thick Vermont woods?

Natasha's mind spins, a dizzying rush of uncertainty. It's a scary moment, the moment you realize you cannot trust your own memories.

When she finally opens her eyes, Adam is gazing down at her with a curious expression. "What are you thinking?"

She shakes her head. She doesn't want to talk about Christopher. Not with Adam. Not here. Here, Christopher does not exist.

"Aren't you tired of all of the lies? All of the deceptions?" Though his voice is gentle, his words hit her

165

hard in the chest.

"I – I can't remember."

"What can't you remember?" His thumb moves from her lower lip to her cheek, stroking gently along her jaw, gently encouraging her.

"Any of it." She searches for one crystalline memory to bring all the rest back in focus, and for the first time, she wishes that she'd kept a diary. But would she have been any more truthful in a diary than in her own, verbal, retellings? "Vermont. Christopher. Madison. I can't remember the order of things."

Opening her eyes, she tries to rearrange her thoughts so that when she speaks, they'll make sense. "You know how when you think about your childhood, it's sometimes hard to tell if something is a real memory, something you remember happening, or if it's something you remember happening through the story someone told you. I don't think I can actually remember my fourth birthday, the one where we played musical chairs, but my parents must have told the story of me crying and locking myself in the bathroom enough times that I feel like I remember it." She shakes her head as Adam continues to peer at her through those thick beautiful eyelashes, encouraging her not with words but with his silence.

"Did we really wait until he'd left his wife?" The question is barely a whisper, as if she doesn't want him to hear. "That's what I tell myself. It's only been four years. But I can't remember."

With a melancholy smile, Adam drops his hand from her face. "Memory has a way of protecting us. Of keeping us safe."

"Forget it. I don't want to talk about it."

She thinks he will push her. That he will ask for more than she is willing or able to give now, and there is a part of her hoping that he will do just that. That he will force her to confront whatever it is she's hiding from. Whatever truth lingers in the shadows, waiting for that first burst of light to illuminate it.

Instead, he steps back and says, "Okay."

Adam walks around her, studying the contents of her desk. The pulp mystery from Christopher. The tea canister filled with pens. The quotation above her desk, misattributed to Oscar Wilde: *Everything in the world is about sex except sex. Sex is about power.* The tokens and talismans of her writing life.

"What's this?"

She turns to see what he's looking at and feels the blood drain from her face. "It's nothing." She reaches for the printed manuscript on her desk, an early draft of *Blackmailed*, but he's quicker than she is. She forgot it was there. How could she have forgotten it was there?

But that is the beauty of the studio. That she never has to clean up, never has to worry about what she's left out in plain view because there's no one who will see it.

When she locked up the other day, it never occurred to her that she would invite Adam here, that she should have hid away more pieces of herself.

"Please, give it back."

He shakes his head as he scans the pages clutched in his hands. "Oh, there's no way I'm giving this back." He sits at the edge of the bed, his feet planted firmly on the ground and grins at Natasha. "Should I read it aloud?"

"No!"

He chuckles. "Don't be embarrassed. You know there

are people who would pay a fortune to get a sneak peek of a Layla Allen book?"

She stares at him, speechless, the playful crinkling of his eyes, the confidence he has sitting there at the foot of her bed like he belongs here, in this room. He reads in silence, his forehead wrinkled in concentration. Carefully, he sets aside the first page and continues reading.

She can't watch. It's like a train wreck. That accident on the side of the road and you want, more than anything, to see the carnage, but at the same time, you don't. You absolutely do not.

She paces nervously and then, when she can't take it, can't take his silence, his concentration, she goes to the kitchen to make coffee, futzing and fiddling impatiently.

When she returns, coffee in one hand, Adam is still reading, his expression unreadable and every second of silence drives her insane.

"Can I have a cigarette?"

He looks up in surprise. "You don't smoke."

"I used to."

"Left jacket pocket," he says, fixing her with a steely look. "But don't make a habit out of it."

She almost doesn't get them. In the end, she takes the cigarette and crawls onto the fire escape. She rolls it between her fingers and sips her coffee. She puts it to her lips, sucking air through it, but after all this, she doesn't light it. She just holds it and pretends.

Why is having a single person read her book so much more disquieting than knowing that there are thousands and thousands of people out there reading her books? Why is this worse than that first dreadful moment when she hits publish and then, seconds later, wonders if she's somehow managed to miss a typo?

A knock on the window startles her and she jumps, nearly dropping the cigarette. Adam peers through the sooty window and she shifts over, watching as he crawls agilely out onto the fire escape. Over his shoulder, she sees her manuscript, the forty pages she's written so far, sitting on the bed.

He sits beside her, their thighs pressed together and lights a cigarette, taking short, quick drags. She glances at him from the corner of her eye, but he doesn't speak. And she can only imagine what he's thinking. For the first time since she started writing smut, there's something at stake and she's terrified that in reading *Blackmailed*, she'll suddenly lose something. What, she isn't certain. But she realizes in this moment that whatever it is, she isn't ready to give up on it.

He stamps out his cigarette and crawls back inside and Natasha follows. Inside, she brushes the dust and dirt from her palms and nervously watches as Adam paces the small space, once more dominating it with his presence and size. Finally, he turns towards her.

"Is that what you want?" He jabs his finger towards the pages left on the bed. "You want me to blackmail you? Tell you I'll ruin your life if you don't fuck me?" She flinches at the anger in his voice. "You want me to force you?"

Nervously, she steps back.

"Fuck you, Natasha!" He runs his hand through his hair, eyes flashing wildly. "Say something!"

"You weren't supposed to read that."

He stalks towards her, closing the distance between them until her ass bumps against her desk and there's nowhere for her to go. His jaw works furiously, his hands clenched at his sides as if he's holding himself back.

"Is this what you want?" He gestures angrily at the manuscript. "Do you want me to force you? Or is this all some game you're playing?"

She shakes her head. "Adam," she starts but he cuts her off.

"Fuck you, Natasha. Fuck you." He turns, his shoulders tensed, reminding Natasha of an animal about to attack. She takes a step towards him, her mind scrambling to think of something to calm him down and then he flips around, coming towards her, nostrils flaring.

"Tell me you don't want me," he demands. "Tell me it doesn't turn you on. Tell me you're happy, really happy, and I'll leave you alone. That you're perfectly content hiding away behind this façade you've constructed. Tell me that the life you're living is the life you've always wanted and mean it. Mean it and I'll walk away. I'll leave you alone. But I don't think you can."

"I'm happy," she says weakly.

He lowers his face, his breath coming in quick bursts. "I don't believe you."

"I'm happy," she says with more conviction this time.

"Bullshit. Tell me you haven't thought about it, haven't imagined what it would be like to have me in your bed. No rules. No lies. Just us and all the kinky sex you've ever dreamed of. I see you, Natasha. Even when you don't see yourself, I see you." He reaches out and for a second, Natasha thinks he's going to touch her cheek, but at the last moment, his hand drops to his side. "One night. Give me one night to prove this is worth something. That it's more than lust. One night and then you can tell me you're happy and I'll walk away. I'll drop your class and you'll never have to see me again."

She grips the desk until her knuckles turn white. The promise in his words makes her entire body tremble. If she's honest, it does more than that. Her nipples are hard and she's wet.

How many times as she thought about it? How many times as she touched herself, thinking of Adam's hands on her?

"One night?"

He nods.

Natasha swallows the lump in her throat. "No sex."

With a wicked grin, Adam steps back. "Not even when you beg."

CHAPTER TWENTY-THREE

One night. That's all she promised him. And she has every intention of keeping her word even as she keeps thinking of telling the taxi driver to turn around, to take her home.

Home. She shivers, trying to banish thoughts of Christopher from her mind. She tells herself she's doing this for them. That she needs answers. That she can't promise him forever if she doesn't know.

She needs to know.

No matter what the cost.

She needs to be certain.

One night. And if she can get through that unscathed, her life will return to what it once was. Simple. Easy. Comfortable.

Boring.

She rests her cheek against the cool glass, letting her eyes close as she tries to ignore the twisting feeling in the pit of her stomach, the pins and needles of uncertainty.

His text gave nothing away. Just an Upper East Side

address and instructions to be there at eight pm, sharp, wearing a dress.

As the taxi slows to a stop, Natasha opens her eyes, finding herself on a quiet tree-lined residential street in the East Sixties. When she sees Adam, leaning against a stunning mansion, his black clothing standing in stark relief against the pearlescent white building, she feels her pulse quicken.

She pays and steps out of the taxi, her heels striking loudly against the sidewalk. Almost loud enough to drown out the sound of her rapidly beating heart or the blood rushing in her ears.

Almost.

She greets him with a nervous smile. One night. That's it. That's all he asked for. And he promised. No sex. She can do this.

But looking at Adam, his perfectly drawn features, the sensual curve of his lips, his broad shoulders and perfectly mussed hair, she knows she is stepping across an invisible line and she wonders if it will ever be possible to go back.

Dropping his cigarette to the ground, Adam pushes off the wall and comes towards her, the graceful movement of his lithe body making her nipples ache and then he's standing before her, snaking one arm around her waist and drawing her to him.

The heat of his body warms her as he dips his head. Natasha closes her eyes, expecting his lips on hers and when they brush against her cheek, disappointment wells up inside her.

"Ready?" he whispers and all the sensual promise of his husky voice washes away her disappointment. She looks up at him, at his eyes glimmering in the darkness and swallows the lump in her throat.

"Yes." It's a lie but it's a necessary one. Adam laughs, stepping back to admire her.

"You look stunning. I thought about bringing you to my apartment. About having you in my bed. But that didn't seem like enough. Though I wonder, with you, if there is ever such a thing as enough."

His words send a ripple of desire through her body.

"Where are we?"

Adam's husky laughter dances across her skin, making her nipples tighten. "Paradise." When she looks at him in obvious confusion, his eyes crinkle with amusement. "Ever been to a play party before?" he asks.

"You're kidding?"

He takes her hand, threading his fingers through hers. "Tell me, Natasha, are you ready?"

One night, she reminds herself, nodding shakily. One night.

A gorgeous young woman dressed as a French maid greets them by the door, taking their coats.

Under the warm light of the foyer, Adam stands taller, the picture of confidence and self-assurance. "Give her your dress."

Natasha nearly balks at the cool command before reminding herself that this is what she agreed to. One night with Adam. One night, handing over control. She turns around and Adam eases down her zipper, teasing the column of her spine with his fingertips.

Her nipples, already hard, begin to ache.

She steps out of her dress and hands it to the French maid. All the while, Adam watches, his eyes lapping up her appearance, the garter and stockings, the four-inch heels, the miniscule g-string and matching shelf bra that lifts her pert breasts but barely covers her nipples.

His expression sends a wave of desire through her.

"Breathtaking," he says at last, reaching into his pocket to retrieve something. "One final touch." He motions her closer. In his hand is a black leather collar. She licks her lips and inclines her head as he snaps it in place, the leather cool and supple against her delicate skin.

He runs one hand across her collarbone, making her heart leap.

"You're more perfect than I even imagined."

Without another word, he takes her hand, guiding her deeper into the lavish mansion. Crystal chandeliers cast a warm glow over intricately laid parquet floors. And there hangs in the air the unmistakable promise of lavish decay, of the final hours of decadence.

Here, in the heart of Manhattan's richest and most illustrious neighborhood, stands a house devoted to sinful pleasure and sensual excess. Men in crisply tailored suits, women in leather and lingerie. Everyone gorgeous. Everyone exuding that ineffable aura of wealth and power.

She follows him down a wide corridor, past open doors, each one a window into a different fantasy. The doctor's office. The executive suite, with a large mahogany desk behind which sits a man, smoking a cigar as he watches a naked woman dust the spotless bookshelves.

"Higher."

With the grace of a dancer, she lifts herself onto the balls of her feet, one arm reaching over head as she dusts.

Natasha has read all about play parties, researching various books, and while she was always tempted, she's never attended one. The ones she read about online all held the stench of seediness, of dark warehouses which she imagined filled with pale, leather clad bodies, their flesh clammy.

This place, whatever it is, never appeared in any of her Google searches.

"What is this place?"

Adam glances over his shoulder. "Paradise," he says with a playful grin.

Natasha pouts. "Come on, that's not all you're going to tell me, is it?"

He strokes her hand with his thumb as he talks. "That's what it's called," he says, shrugging. "A woman named Jax runs it. Very exclusive. Lots of money. Absolute secrecy. Those are her rules. Otherwise, almost anything goes."

"How long have you been coming here?"

He grins but doesn't respond, stopping only when they come to a curved staircase. Up or down? She feels like Alice in Wonderland. Drink the potion. The world will never be the same.

A small bronze plaque next to the staircase is engraved with a single word DUNGEON and an arrow pointing down.

"Come." Adam tugs on her hand, leading her upstairs and away from the promise of the dungeon. "There's something I want to show you first."

Up another flight of stairs, Natasha's mind racing, each step they take making her anticipation build to a near breaking point.

On the top floor of the mansion, silence reigns and Adam leads her through a set of double doors and into an ornate library. Mahogany and books. Rich, sumptuous leather and soft Persian rugs that swallow up the sound of her steps.

A naked woman sits in a leather club chair, her legs drawn up, reading, as if it is the most normal thing in the world.

Adam snaps his fingers impatiently and the woman, upon seeing him, jumps to her feet, clasping her hands behind her back, her head bowed as Natasha watches on in amazement.

She feels like she has stepped into an alternate universe she thought existed only in books.

"Sasha, get us drinks."

With an almost imperceptible nod, the woman leaves, her naked body breathtaking in the dim light of the library, and Natasha glances at Adam, seeing him as if for the first time. What secrets does he keep? And what would she be willing to do to unravel them?

The thought unnerves her.

"You said you keep your writing a secret so your parents won't find out," Adam says, wandering purposefully towards the far wall of books. "But is that the only reason?" Amongst the collection of books, Natasha recognizes many of the names on the spines. Sade. Réage. Roquelaure. "Or is there a part of you that's ashamed to write about sex? To dedicate yourself to something that so many people see as dirty or trivial?" Adam gently probes. "I fell in love with Layla Allen because she is fearless. She doesn't care what people think. She doesn't censor herself. All that matters to her is pleasure. And pain."

When Adam lifts her hand, pointing to a shelf, she sees it. An entire row of her books. It isn't just seeing them, but seeing them here, in this beautiful, miraculous library, that makes her breath catch and her chest tighten painfully. She takes a step forward. She's always imagined them, dinged up paperbacks on someone's nightstand or lost amidst a sea of other dinged up paperbacks. Here, in this church to smut, housed amongst the great writers of the genre, they look important. Part of the history. Part of the narrative.

She hears the door open but doesn't take her eyes off the books. Her books. The experience is unexpected and profound and she needs a minute to process what she's feeling. Finally, Adam places his hand on her back, turning her gently.

There, standing in the threshold, is a woman dressed all in black, her head held high, her grey eyes burning with curiosity.

Though there's nothing overtly frightening about her, Natasha senses her power in the confident way that she holds herself.

"Jax."

The woman smiles and crosses the room, taking Natasha's hand and lifting it to her lips. "You must be the beautiful Layla. Adam didn't exaggerate."

Natasha's head snaps towards Adam but Jax's cool voice draws her back again.

"Don't be upset. You wouldn't be here if he hadn't told me." The fondness in Jax's voice is evident. "I've wanted to meet you for some time."

Jax sinks into the armchair, her posture perfect yet relaxed, and motions to the chair opposite her. Obediently, Natasha takes her seat, sitting up straight, the leather against her thighs making her suddenly aware of her nakedness, unable to shake the feeling that she has been called to the principal's office to be reprimanded.

"Adam has told me a lot about you," she begins, lifting her glass to her lips to sip the amber liquid. "I promise you, your secret is safe with me. I do not betray confidences." Her steely gaze doesn't waver and Natasha shivers suddenly. "We all have secrets, some more open than others, some more dangerous than others. Do you think the hedge fund where I work knows about all this?" Her grey eyes twinkle with amusement. "Do you have any idea how many CEOs of Fortune 500 companies like to unwind after a long day by having a woman beat them black and blue? Their secrets are my secrets and here, they are safe to do as they please, knowing that no one will judge them by their private fantasies.

"But men do not understand secrets as women do. They fear their masculinity being questioned. But women, women know the true value of secrets and so, while I admire your work, I disagree with Adam's belief that you should be open about it. Men like to think they know what's best, but there is no way for a man who is the embodiment of all that patriarchy holds dear to understand the inherent risks of possessing ovaries."

Her voice is thoughtful and hypnotic.

"Not long ago, a woman I knew was outed. It was a very regrettable thing. She was a school teacher who adored her students, fourth graders I think, but someone found out that she enjoyed certain, shall we say, unconventional pleasures on her own time. The result was tragic. She will never teach again."

Jax holds Natasha's gaze, silently conveying a warning without the need for words. Once satisfied she understands, Jax turns to Adam, smiling. "Did you show her the etchings?"

Adam shakes his head. "We just got here."

She laughs. "Oh, don't be like that." Jax comes to her feet and wanders across the room, glancing over her shoulder to beckon Natasha.

She points to a framed sketch on the wall. The image, done in clean pen strokes, is of a woman with her hands tied together with a rope tossed over a tree branch. Beneath it, the words, In the garden, I was taken. I regret nothing except that it did not happen sooner.

Natasha turns quickly towards Jax, who is smiling at her. "Daniel Picard is an old friend and quite a fan of your work." She sips her drink thoughtfully. "I'll have a copy sent to you. Adam has your address, no?"

Natasha looks back at the sketch. The image, in stark pen, is one that she created. But seeing it seen through someone else's eyes does something that she cannot define. For a moment, she forgets even her nakedness.

She feels an overwhelming sense of gratitude towards the woman standing beside her. "Thank you." The words do not begin to convey the feelings rioting inside Natasha.

"I hope you understand that you cannot write about this place. A breach of such trust…" Jax shakes her head sadly, but the threat is clear. But just as quickly, she smiles. "I would like to ask a favor of you."

Natasha stares at her in amazement, the way she jumps from one subject to the next, the way she can make the most innocent words sound menacing…

"Of course."

"Good. It would amuse some of my —" Jax pauses, "associates, greatly, if you might dedicate a book to me. I understand, of course, if that's asking too much." She blinks her large grey eyes and Natasha can only nod, knowing that though Jax has posed this as a question, it carries the weight of an order.

"Fantastic!" Jax clasps her hands together in delight, giving Natasha a peculiar vertiginous feel. "Now, I'll leave you two alone. Natasha, it's been a sincere pleasure to meet you. I hope that you enjoy your evening and that we will be seeing more of you in the future."

Natasha breathlessly watches the woman slip from the room, letting the door close softly in her wake. And only then does she sag with relief and realize that she's shaking.

Her mouth feels sticky, her tongue heavy. She can't shake the feeling that Jax was assessing her, and her threat, subtle, artful, lingers in the air like perfume.

Adam grasps her shoulders, spinning her towards him. She sees in his eyes arousal and playful humor and she forgets Jax. Forgets everything but this god of a man in front of her.

He trails his index finger over the swell of her breasts, making her quiver with expectation. "I think it's time to show you the dungeon."

CHAPTER TWENTY-FOUR

Adam stops abruptly, the double doors behind him all that stand between them and the dungeon.

"Do you trust me?" He searches her face for hesitation or doubt but there is none. Only scorching curiosity.

Whatever his intention for showing her the library, she left feeling stronger and more certain.

"Yes," Natasha says firmly.

"Pick a safe word."

Her eyebrows arch. She's never needed a safe word before and she's confident she won't need one now. She trusts Adam implicitly, trusts that he knows what he's doing and that he won't push her too far. But the determined set of his jaw makes her realize that no matter how much she trusts him now, he won't let her through those doors until she's settled on a safe word.

"Red," she says.

For a long while, Adam just stares at her and when he finally reaches out, cupping her face, she leans into his palm, into the comfort of his touch. Gently, he brushes his lips over hers.

"Ready?"

"Absolutely."

With a grin, Adam pushes open the doors, stepping aside to let her enter first. Her eyes widen as moans of pleasure and pain rise to greet them. Adam stands wordlessly beside her as she rapidly moves her head, eyes darting around the spacious room, trying to capture every detail, trying to memorize every sight and sound and smell. The man kneeling at the feet of a beautiful woman dressed head to toe in leather. The woman bent over a spanking bench as another woman casually strokes her pussy while talking to a man. Voices, subdued, carry through the large open space, adding to the sense that they are underwater.

"This could be yours. Ours." Adam spreads his hands. "Every fantasy. Every desire. Everything you've ever written about, everything you've ever wanted. All you have to do is say yes."

Adam leads the way, Natasha following behind him, the sounds of her heels hitting the tiled floor swallowed up in the cavernous room. A woman tied in place, a vibrator lodged between her legs. Her moans, of pleasure and torment, make Natasha flush.

A man like a blond Viking approaches her and runs his hand between her legs, fondling her roughly, drawing moans from the woman.

"Don't you dare come," he orders through clenched teeth and the woman stills, fighting the orgasm so clearly building inside of her. Natasha catches his cruel smile and knows the woman has no chance. The man will guarantee she fails.

Her flesh ripples. Her hips subtly humping the

whipping post. She tries to fight it, tries to mask the inevitable, but a sharp moan pierces the room as her hips buck.

The man, chuckling, says, "I told you not to come," as he reaches for a leather paddle. The woman screams.

Natasha is awed. Aroused. It feels like a door has opened onto the darkest corners of her mind. Here, in this room, she can be anyone she wants to be. Without apology or remorse.

Consciously or not, she is aware of the way even her gait has changed, the provocative sway of her hips.

Here, it is impossible to deny that they are carnal beings.

Adam leads her through the room, pausing so she can take it all in.

"This is marvelous," she whispers, admiring a St. Andrew's Cross on a small, empty stage.

"After you." He holds out his hand, motioning for her to step up onto the stage. Natasha shudders. This, now, is what she agreed to.

Everything else was foreplay.

She glances over her shoulder, biting her lip. "No sex."

Who is she reminding?

"No sex," he promises with an arrogant smile. Natasha refuses to be disappointed by his easy acquiescence, instead, turning back to the saltire and running her fingers over the burnished wood, gleaming warmly beneath the overhead lights. Smooth. Hard. Unblemished. It's a work of art, carefully crafted, beautifully designed.

"Have you ever been tied to the cross before?"

The unexpected closeness of Adam's voice makes her jump. "No." She shakes her head.

"I like the idea of being your first." He presses against her, making her acutely aware of every place their bodies come into contact.

He begins at her hips, hands caressing, teasing, his fingers ghosting across her skin as he moves upwards, cupping her firm breasts, cradling them in the palms of his hands. "You have no idea how many times I've dreamed of having you here. Of touching you. Having you at my mercy. Making you scream."

Arousal, hot and muscular tightens around her, making it hard to breathe.

"I've thought about fucking you as the whole room watches," he says, nipping at her neck. "I've imagined whipping you until your skin is hot and red and marked. I've imagined the look on your face when I let you come."

Natasha moans when he steps away, breaking the connection, yanking her back to the present. With an impatient tug, he releases her bra, freeing her breasts.

"You won't be needing this," he says, letting her bra fall to the floor. He fondles her breasts in his large, warm hands, rolling her nipples between his able fingers. Her head falls back against his chest as she sinks deeper and deeper into this moment, into his arms.

Pleasure devours her whole.

Arousal consumes her.

Roughly, he flips her around so that they stand facing one another. He leans in and she imagines his lips on hers, but at the last moment, chuckling, he turns away and she is left panting, wanting what he denied her.

He keeps his eyes on her as he lifts one of her arms and then she feels the stiff leather cuff tighten around her wrist, fastening her in place. Hands dance across her collarbones, fingers teasing her flesh until even the hairs at her nape stand to attention.

"Are you scared?"

"No." Natasha laughs nervously. "Okay, maybe a little."

"It's okay to be scared," he says, deftly locking her other arm to the cross. His steady voice calms her. "Breathe. You're safe. I promise."

His lips burn their way down her body. Natasha squeezes her eyes shut, desperately gasping for breath as he moves lower. Her belly jumps as his thumbs graze her hips then hook beneath her g-string, drawing it down with tantalizing slowness, exposing her to his hungry gaze. With a shuddering breath, she steps out of it and Adam catches her ankle, bringing his lips to the top of her foot.

He kneels at her feet, his breath hot and moist where it meets her flesh, sending goose bumps across her skin.

"No marks. Nothing I'll have to explain." She trembles as she feels her control slipping away.

"Of course."

As Adam edges her legs open, spreading her sex for him, she realizes that it was not hubris that caused him to say she would beg him to fuck her but self awareness.

She stands before him, arms spread above her head, in nothing but silk stockings and a black lace garter belt. With shocking efficiency, he cuffs her ankles to the cross.

This is it.

Total surrender.

Spread wide for Adam and the entire room to see.

"Safe word?" he asks, his voice serious, as he comes to his feet.

"Red." The word comes out shaky and uncertain.

"Good girl."

He leans into her, hands pressing her hands into the wood, and sucks her earlobe into his mouth. "Are you turned on?" he whispers roughly.

"Yes." His erection presses against her abdomen, hard, thick, insistent.

"Good."

He steps away, leaving her gasping for more, lost in the swirl of desire. No marks. No sex. What does that leave? But watching Adam move confidently across the stage, she has no doubt that he'll make the most of their one night together, no matter what the restrictions.

One night.

What if it isn't enough?

The thought sends a wave of panic crashing over her. Christopher, at home, who thinks she is spending the night with an old college friend. Christopher, who loves her so much it's sometimes physically painful.

The light tap of a crop against her inner thigh brings her sharply back to the present.

"Focus," Adam breathes into her ear. "Open your eyes." He taps the riding crop against her inner thigh again.

Swallowing her panic, Natasha obeys and when she does, she gasps. Standing in small groups at the foot of the stage are people, strangers, their eyes riveted on her, watching them, watching her. She is a show. A diversion.

Her mouth goes dry.

Adam's hands continue their exploration. Down her sides. Down her legs. Up again. Her sex, opened wide, pulsing with need, aching for attention. He crouches before her, breathing her in.

"Should I taste you?" he whispers. "Should I lick your

pussy until you scream?"

"Yes," Natasha whispers, realizing now that he will punish her not with pain but by making her admit all that she wants from him. All that she's denied until this moment. "Please."

"Please what?" His lips twitch with barely concealed amusement.

"Please, *sir.*"

He laughs, the vibrations running down her spine. "I can't hear you."

"Please, sir, lick my pussy." Her lips remain parted. Adam grins up at her.

"Now that I have you here, I never want to let you go," he declares, devouring her with his eyes. "I want to tease you and lick you and fuck you until you collapse and then I want to do it all over again. I want to make you beg me to fuck you and then I want you begging me to stop because you don't think you'll survive one more orgasm. I want to destroy you with my cock and heal you with my mouth. I want to live and die between your thighs. I want you to submit to me in a room filled with people so you can watch the way they look at you, the jealousy in their eyes knowing you belong to me."

Tied to the cross, Natasha can only accept his words, accept the rare touches he grants her. Everything else disappears. All that's left is his voice, mesmerizing her, captivating, his presence, his touch. She sees the desire burning in his eyes, hears it in his deep husky voice and it makes the blood rush to her head.

His hot breath on her neck as he kisses along her jaw, working his way towards her mouth. He grips her ass in his hands, his fingers bruising as they clutch her flesh. Her lips part in invitation and he chuckles as his tongue darts out, licking along her lower lip, tasting her, the briefest taste that leaves Natasha groaning in frustration.

"I want to hear you cry out for me. I want my name to be the last thing you scream before you come. On my cock. On my lips. On my fingers. I want your body. Your mind. Your submission. I've never wanted anything the way I want you. We were made for each other." He steps closer. "You know that, don't you?"

Her skin ripples with pleasure and he has barely even touched her. She can only nod.

"I want your orgasms, your desires, your passions. I want to inspire you. To be the reason you run out of bed in the morning to write. And then the reason you run back to bed at night. I want you screaming as I run my cock over your clit, begging me to fuck you."

The scent of her arousal fills Natasha's nostrils. No one has spoken to her like this before. No one has made her feel this alive and this out of control. His lips on her flesh make her ache. When his wet mouth closes around her nipple, her back arches despite her bonds.

She wants this.

She needs this.

She burns for this.

He bites into her sensitive nipple, eliciting a sound barely human from somewhere deep inside of her and then he releases it, licking his tongue over her skin, lapping the sweat from her flesh. He moves slowly down her trembling body, down her belly, pressing his lips to the hollow of her hip, kissing her belly button, his tongue swirling, dancing, as she yanks at her bonds.

He kneels before her spread legs and no man has ever

looked as powerful as Adam looks kneeling in front of her. He glances up, eyes glassy and dark, filled with emotions Natasha cannot ever hope to decode. All she knows is that she needs more.

She needs Adam.

She needs everything he has promised her and more.

When he kisses her inner thigh, she feels the wetness between her legs, her sex tightening in frustration.

He grins. "Tell me you want this. Tell me you need this."

"I need this," she whispers, shuddering. "I need you. Please."

"Say my name." He runs his tongue along her inner thigh, making Natasha quiver with desire.

"Adam," she moans and then his tongue is on her sex, his mouth hot and passionate as he devours her. Her back spasms. Her body clenches with pleasure. "Adam. Adam. Adam," she repeats his name like a prayer, a supplication as he licks her pussy hungrily and then he slides a finger into her, stretching her, teasing her, finding the exact spot that makes her body tense and her mind blank. Pleasure coils deep inside her belly, her orgasm glimmering in the distance. She rocks her hips as much as the cuffs allow.

When he leans back onto his heels, watching her, fucking her with his fingers, her mind stills.

"I want you to need me as much as I need you."

"I need you."

"How much?" His fingers slow, his touch teasing and Natasha whimpers.

"More than anything."

When their eyes meet, nothing else exists.

He presses harder with his fingers, his tongue returning

to her clit as he eats her with such wild abandon Natasha can only throw back her head and let it all wash over her.

She comes. Bucking and screaming, her orgasm threatening to rip her apart.

His fingers never stop. His tongue never stops. Her hips buck wildly, the delicious pleasure painful.

"Adam, please," she begs without knowing what she's begging for.

When he leans back, she sees her arousal glistening on his lips and when his tongue darts from his mouth, licking it up, she feels it in her chest.

"What do you want, Natasha?" he asks, coming to his feet and before she has a chance to respond, his lips are on hers, a bruising kiss that proves his dominance. She sags into her restraints, letting him take her, taste her, take care of her.

His erection digs into her belly, a hard reminder of all that she wants but cannot have.

What she wouldn't do to feel it inside her.

And when Adam breaks away, panting, his dark eyes dilated with arousal, she wants nothing more than to feel his erection filling her, making her his.

The words hover on her lips but she can't bring herself to say them. She sees in his eyes the proud determination of a man in control and she realizes, struggling for breath, that he isn't done.

Not by a long shot.

He's just getting started.

She swallows hard, wondering if she'll survive the night. Slowly, she becomes aware of the room around them, the crowd of people standing at the foot of the platform, watching them, watching their performance. Jax, standing among them, with a hint of a smile. Beside her, Sasha kneels, her legs spread, her eyes locked on Natasha, while Jax strokes her hair, the absent-minded gesture of a woman with her pet.

Natasha looks away, her eyes returning to Adam, powerful, beautiful Adam, Adam who has promised her the world, who has promised to make her every fantasy a reality.

He cocks his head, considering her, his jaw set, his expression unreadable. And Natasha, in this moment, wonders what magical experiences she might have with him, if only she says yes. If only she agrees.

But what would she be agreeing to?

With a wicked grin, he turns his back to her, jogging down the steps, his muscles flexing beneath his shirt. He says something to Jax and Jax glances at Natasha, her grey eyes boring into her, before nodding to Adam.

With a snap of Jax's fingers, Sasha comes to her feet, her head bowed deferentially as she stands before Adam. Natasha wishes, more than anything, that she could hear what Adam is saying. For a moment, the girl lifts her eyes, glancing at Natasha, and then she pads barefoot across the room, disappearing from sight.

When Adam returns to the stage, Natasha is shaking. The strength of her orgasm, the heat of their connection, and now, she is shivering.

"There's so much I want to do to you tonight. So much I want to show you," he says and she can hear the passion in his voice.

"Show me," she says without considering the consequences. "Show me everything."

"Are you sure?"

"No. But do it anyway."

He laughs, a low rumble she can feel all the way to her toes. She barely notices the girl come up on the stage and hand a heavy briefcase to Adam. He takes it, thanking her, and she melts back into the crowd.

He sets it on a small table and clicks it open. Natasha strains her neck, trying to see, but held in place, she sees nothing but Adam's strong back. He returns to her, and her eyes dart between his face and his hands. In one, he holds a sleek metal vibrator. In the other, a long tailed flogger.

Desire pools in her belly.

"Which shall it be?" he asks, teasing.

Natasha chews her lip. "Both. Everything. I want it all."

Adam grins. "That's my girl. Greedy. Insatiable. Wild. Close your eyes."

She does, her eyelashes brushing her cheek as she shivers with anticipation.

"How many orgasms do you think I can give you before the night is out? How many orgasms until you beg me to stop?"

Her lips part. The world dissolves. She is a body. She is sensation. She is this moment and she hopes it never ends.

"However many you'd like, sir," she says finally, falling into a role she feels was written just for her.

The smooth suede tails lick across her belly, making her muscles jump. Adam's low chuckle ripples across her skin.

With a flick of his wrist, he brings them down on her clit, making her gasp. "Let's say five, shall we?" The buzz of the vibrator is the last thing Natasha hears before it touches her and all rational thought melts away, replaced with pleasure.

CHAPTER TWENTY-FIVE

Spent, Natasha collapses into his strong arms. With ease, Adam lifts her, cradling her to his chest and she buries her face against him, inhaling the scent of him.

His arms tighten around her body as he makes his way from the room and Natasha burrows deeper into him, feeling weightless. She doesn't care where he takes her as long as he remains with her.

She finally opens her eyes when he eases her onto a bed. She blinks, drinking him in, pure masculine perfection standing at the foot of the bed, his erection clearly drawn through his jeans, his jaw tight, his eyes dark.

She stretches her arms above her, weightless, listless, noticing at last the ache of her muscles. She is naked except for her garter and stockings, her thighs slippery. She shivers. On the cross, everything felt surreal. Now, here, in this bedroom decorated in white and pale blue, reality begins to seep in.

She sits up, grabbing a pillow and hugging it to her chest.

Adam's eyes darken. "Turn around," he says, his voice tight, gruff.

"Adam, what are you doing?"

"After care," he says tightly. "Turn around."

She scoots around, facing the headboard, still clutching the pillow to her chest. The mattress dips as Adam gets onto the bed behind her. She feels his heat against her naked back and then his strong able fingers are massaging her sore, aching muscles. With a moan, she melts into him, once more relinquishing control.

Her eyelids flutter. His erection presses into her, a reminder of everything he gave her, everything he took from her, and everything she has yet to give him.

She wants him.

Wants him more than anything in the world.

Wants to give him even a fraction of what he's given her.

"Natasha," he says in a gruff whisper. "There's not a chance in hell I'm letting you go after tonight." He sucks in a sharp breath. "I love you. I love everything about you. And that's never going to change."

Her spine stiffens. "Adam," she squeaks in panic.

"Hush. Just listen." His fingers dig painfully into the tight muscles of her shoulders. "I love you. Fight this, fight me, but that's never changing. But after tonight, how can you keep denying this? Denying how I make you feel?"

She hears the faint undercurrent of anger in his voice. The accusation. The recriminations but his able fingers never stop massaging her aching muscles, providing relief. And his erection stays lodged between them, a cruel reminder. A taunt.

"You don't even know me," she whispers, blinking

back tears.

"Bullshit. How can you even say that?" She tries to pull away, but Adam's large hands lock her in place, trapping her. Tears sting her eyes and she blinks rapidly.

"Christopher is the one who doesn't know you. Christopher is the one who only thinks he knows you. I know you. I see you. Let me see you, Natasha. Let me see you. And I promise, you won't regret it."

Pain radiates through her, a deep ugly pain with no physical cause. This time, when she pulls away, he lets her and she spins around, pulling her legs up to her chest to hide her nakedness as she stares at him. His face is tense, his eyes searching.

"That's not fair," she whispers, feeling suddenly very small and fragile.

His jaw twitches. "There's no such thing as fair."

A single hot tear rolls down her cheek as she opens her mouth to speak but no words come out. She stares at him in stunned silence.

"Walk away and you'll spend the rest of your life wondering what might have happened. What could have been."

Tears cloud her vision and Natasha gulps in air. This isn't supposed to happen. He isn't supposed to love her. It feels like the walls are closing in, like the air is thinning. Her hands fly to her neck, fingers clawing at the leather collar she's still wearing. Adam gingerly pulls her hands away and unfastens it, letting it fall to the mattress.

The look he gives her makes her say the one thing she knows will put an end to his demands. "He asked me to marry him."

For a split second, Adam doesn't react and then, as the

words hit home, he recoils. "When?"

"In London. Before the semester started."

After a few moments of stunned silence, he finally speaks. "What did you say?"

Natasha chews her lip, the tears coming faster, hotter, splashing onto the bed between them. "I said I'd think about it."

"It's a mistake and you know it."

She shakes her head, her eyebrows bunching together. "Don't."

"Admit it. It's a mistake," he says hotly. "If you wanted to marry him, you would have said yes. But you didn't."

She shakes. "Please, stop. Please," she begs, sobbing.

He gets off the bed, pacing the room, and she hugs her legs tighter, afraid he'll hit something, that he'll take his anger out on one of the vases on the side table as tension rolls off him.

At last, he stops and turns to her.

His eyes burn into her.

"Don't marry him."

Beneath his rough demand, she hears the vulnerability, the plea and it's that devastating hope that makes her drop her head to her chest and let out a sob. Cursing, Adam gets back onto the bed, wrapping his arms around her, hushing her, telling her not to worry, telling her that everything will be okay.

As he rocks her in his arms, she tries to believe him. But she can't.

Natasha knows the truth.

Whatever happens, everything will *not* be okay.

CHAPTER TWENTY-SIX

In the hazy grey light of dawn, Natasha eases out of Adam's sleeping arms, dragging her aching body from the warm bed.

Looking down at him, the gentle rise and fall of his chest, the way his long, lean body is still curled as it was around her body, she has to fight the urge to brush his hair from his face.

Reluctantly, she turns away, finding her clothing folded on the dresser. She dresses in silence, afraid that if she wakes him, she'll never leave this room, that the desire to remain here, with Adam, will outshine everything else.

With a final glance, she steals into the hallway. The house, so alive the night before, is silent in the early hours. Images from last night flash in her mind, making her chest tighten painfully.

She steps out onto the street and sucks in a breath. The city, bathed in a soft grey light, feels like a dream. Too still to be real. As Natasha makes her way uptown to her studio, past closed stores, the only evidence of life is the delivery trucks idling at the curb.

Even her studio, when she finally arrives, feels changed by the occurrences of the night before. She sinks to her bed, staring at her hands on her lap, remembering the feel of Adam's hands on her body, the way she writhed beneath his touch.

What the hell did she do?

The orgasms ripped from her body. The crowd of onlookers. The freedom of absolute surrender.

And then, afterwards, when she was still weak from all he had taken and all he had given, Adam's unexpected confession. How could he do that? How could he put her in that position?

Her anger is directed as much at herself as it is at Adam. Did she really think, all this time, that all that existed between them was lust?

But it was easier to believe that. Easier to believe that Adam, for all this seductive words, wanted nothing more than her body.

As long as she sits here, all she'll be able to do is replay it over and over again. His expression. His words. Her reckless desire. To risk everything, just for a taste of whatever Adam might give her.

She tries not to think about Christopher because it's too painful. Too difficult to admit, even in the stillness of early morning, that maybe it's really over.

She forces herself to her desk, her shoulders aching, a cruel reminder of everything that happened.

Arousal clenches at her gut, painful, muscular, unavoidable.

She opens *Blackmailed*. Outside, pigeons coo on the windowsill. She knows that finishing the book will accomplish nothing, but she has always thought best while writing, working through the problems with words and so, she puts off going home a little longer, and in these quiet stolen hours as New York City sleeps, she writes.

"Did you expect me to make it that easy? To tell you what to do?" His cruel laughter, like nails scratching her skin, makes her flinch away.

"No, sir."

"You fight me, but you don't mean it. Whenever you say no, we both know you're really saying yes."

She shakes her head, refusing to admit that he's right. He stalks towards her, towering over her, making her back away hastily.

"You wanted me to take you. From the very beginning. That night in Geneva, I didn't force you. You came willingly, begging me to make you forget your sad little suburban life. The domestic squabbles that filled your days. And now you want me to take the blame?" His hand darts out, grabbing her face. He presses his thumb and forefinger into her cheeks, forcing her lips open. "You claim your innocence when the truth is you're nothing but an insatiable whore. I'm just the excuse you needed to live out your darkest desires." His fingers press down as she tries to shake her head. He won't let her. "Does he satisfy you sexually? Does he make you come with the same ferocity that I do? Does he make you wild enough to draw blood?"

His words fill her with horror.

"Say it and maybe I'll let you go. Admit you're an insatiable sex slave. My insatiable little sex slave, and I'll consider having mercy on you."

His eyes burn into her. Eyes of a devil. Eyes of a god. She wants to spit in his face. She wants to kick him. Wants to make him bleed the way he's made her bleed.

Instead, she licks her lips, watching the self-satisfied smirk that passes across his face as she says, "I'm your insatiable little sex slave."

A sob rips through her body as his sinister laughter fills her ears. "I know," he says, patting her cheek with unexpected tenderness. "I know."

Natasha sits back in disgust. For a moment, brief and pressing, she considers erasing it all. Command + A. Command + C. That's all it would take. Two key strokes to erase the evidence of her infidelity.

Her fingers hover over the keyboard.

The devil on her shoulder screams at her to do it.

Or is it the angel?

But Natasha can't even do that.

Her hands fall away and her head drops to her chest. Closing her eyes, she sees Adam, standing in the bedroom at the mansion and his pained expression when she told him Christopher asked her to marry him.

No one forced her to tell him. She did it to hurt him. To make him feel just a little of the pain he caused her.

The moment the words were out, she regretted them. Regretted betraying Christopher by telling Adam. Regretted hurting Adam out of spite.

Her eyes sting. She looks at the computer, half wishing that the Adam she knows was even half as cruel as the Alex she's written.

"I didn't mean to hurt you." Her voice, quiet, fragile, echoes in the empty room and she doesn't know, even as she says the words, if they are meant for Christopher or for Adam.

How will she face Christopher when she gets home? He'll be sitting there on the couch, in plaid flannel pajamas, sipping coffee out of his favorite mug, the one she bought him their first Christmas together, just a silly mug from a museum in London.

The moment he hears her key in the lock, he'll look up, setting aside the newspaper, his blue eyes wide with tenderness and love.

He loves her.

But does he know her?

Would he love her just the same if he did?

The answer is unknowable.

Was Adam right? Or was he throwing rocks, a petulant child hoping to make her bleed?

But the look on his face when he said it wasn't anger. It wasn't the face of a man lashing out violently. No, instead, he looked at her like a disappointed parent.

How can you compromise your life for him? Your integrity?

Even if she tells him the truth, about Layla Allen, about the books she writes, about the things she wants, won't she be compromising herself to be with him?

And the question Natasha can't answer, the question she knows she must answer: Is it worth it?

Is Christopher worth that sacrifice? All love requires sacrifice and compromise, but how much of yourself are you expected to give up? How much of yourself *can* you give up before you become someone else, someone you no longer recognize?

Her face twists in pain as she fights back the tears, knowing she has no right to cry. Not after last night.

She may not have slept with Adam but that hardly lessens her betrayal.

How could she do this?

To Christopher.

To Adam.

How could she be so selfish?

Pain courses through her and she grits her teeth, fighting past it. She feels like she's drowning. Like she is being crushed beneath some terrible weight.

She wonders if the decision was made a long time ago, a million tiny choices that add up to something life shattering. That she is merely postponing the inevitable, working up the courage to act, all the while drawing out the pain for everyone involved, herself included.

With renewed determination, she returns to her computer, knowing that she must finish this. That she must see it through to the end.

He stares into her soul.

"What will your husband say when I show him the pictures?"

Natalia's face pales as she imagines her husband seeing the images, her naked on the bed, her hungry expression as he dangles his cock over her open mouth.

It will break him. It will destroy him.

The cruelty of it makes her skin crawl.

The cruelty of it makes her wet.

"You wouldn't," she says at last, stepping forward, surprising Alex.

"Try me."

For the first time, she understands the game they've been playing and it makes her smile.

"Show him and I'm free. I'll have nothing left to lose. Nothing left for you to ruin." She takes another step, closing the distance between them. Her breath comes in short puffs. "Show him," she says, jabbing her finger at his chest. "Show him! Ruin me! I want you to ruin me!"

Alex steps back, his eyes widening, which only makes her laugh, a wild, maniacal laugh of someone on the verge of insanity.

It is the laugh of someone with nothing to lose.

Alex, who moments before held the power in his hands, now stares at her like an unpredictable stranger. Like she is dangerous.

Wiping away her tears, she smiles at him, and her smile, though sweet, is razor sharp. "That's what I thought. You don't want me ruined." She shakes her head in disgust, a taste like pennies filling her mouth. Her lips twist into a sneer as she opens her arms wide. "I'm your insatiable little whore. I'm your pussy. I'm yours."

Natasha closes her computer, switches off her cell phone, and heads home. Her secret, which once felt so vital, so important, now, in the face of everything else, feels merely inconsequential.

CHAPTER TWENTY-SEVEN

A part of her hopes that when she steps through the front door, Christopher will demand to know where she was and who she was with. That he will look at her and see some sign, some indication of deception.

She wants his accusations. His anger. His pain. Anything but his unconditional love. Anything but his infinite understanding.

Standing in the hallway outside their door, she hesitates, her fingers clenched around her keys. She can't live like this. Can't live with the lies and half-truths.

Finally, when she cannot postpone it any longer, she unlocks the door, stepping into the apartment like a woman about to face the executioner.

But the executioner exists only in her mind. Christopher is just where she imagined him, sitting on the couch, reading the newspaper, the mug she gave him resting on the coffee table, the air tinged with the scent of freshly brewed coffee.

"How was your night?" he asks, setting aside his paper

and Natasha knows in that moment that he's only being polite, that he doesn't actually want to know about her night and that realization makes her want to hurl the truth at him.

"It was nice," she says instead, slipping out of her shoes and padding across the room. Christopher opens his arms, and she sits on his lap.

"Did you have fun?"

She hesitates. "Yeah," she says at last, realizing that, despite everything, it's the truth.

"Good." He hugs her to him and Natasha rests her head against his chest, feeling the familiar comfort of Christopher's embrace, his body warming her, soothing her.

Is she willing to give this up? And for what? For whips and toys and kinky sex? For a man who claims to love her?

Is that enough?

Is she willing to sacrifice the comfort she has for the chance at something else? Something more exciting?

She buries her face in Christopher's neck, inhaling the scent of him, not wanting to let him see her pained expression.

She wonders, sadly, if there is any such thing as enough.

Christopher strokes her back and she can tell that his mind has already moved on.

She avoids her phone, knowing that Adam will not let her off the hook so easily.

He will demand from her the truth, whatever that may be. He will make her say it, aloud.

By Monday afternoon, the party and everything that

happened there feels like a dream. As she sits behind her desk, waiting for her students to arrive, she wonders if she invented it. A scene in a book to keep her mind off her life.

But whenever she thinks about Adam, the tightness in her throat reminds her it was real. So very real.

Now, she must face the consequences.

When the door opens, Natasha stiffens and then, when Adam steps inside, his head down, lost in thought, her worry turns to full on panic.

In the brief moment before he looks up, she allows herself the pleasure of admiring him, the serene beauty of a man aware of his own strength.

And then, just as quickly, the moment is gone. Adam looks up, their eyes meeting, and he freezes. She notices the dark circles under his eyes, the rough stubble along his jaw and it makes her heart ache.

She never wanted to hurt anyone. Seeing Adam now, she realizes the naïveté of such an ambition.

"Natasha," he says, coming forward as if awoken from a spell. He runs one hand through his hair and then, as if realizing what he's doing, he stops, shoving his hand into the back pocket of his jeans.

For the first time since they met, Adam looks uncertain and this change in him affects her deeply. She leans forward, drawn to him, wanting more than anything to ease the pain she sees so clearly in his face.

"Adam," she starts, breaking off when the door opens.

"Hey, Professor Carson," Colin says with a cheerful smile, sliding into his seat and unzipping his backpack.

Natasha glances at Adam, his jaw twitching and she knows that he is just as irritated by the interruption as she is.

They have a lot to discuss.

The problem is, she still doesn't know what to say to him.

"After class," he mouths before turning and taking his seat.

Natasha takes a book out of her bag and pretends to read. The words on the page swim before her eyes and when the rest of her students finally arrive, she sets the book aside, for once relieved to be starting class.

"Okay, who wants to tell me what they thought about 'The Model'?"

Adam waits outside the classroom, leaning against the wall, his hands shoved in his pockets. Somehow he manages to imbue even this casual stance with frustration and impatience.

Wordlessly, Natasha heads for the stairs and Adam falls in beside her. They walk in tense silence, their legs moving quickly as they make their way from the undergraduate humanities building where class is held to the graduate writing department, where Natasha keeps her office.

Natasha's fingers tremble as she unlocks the door to her office.

The moment they get inside, Adam shuts the door angrily and grabs her by the wrist, pulling her towards him, yanking her off balance. Startled, she stumbles into his chest and Adam's arm darts around her, catching her, anchoring her to him.

For a brief moment, she allows herself the comfort of his touch. But when she looks up, the tension in his face and the barely contained fury makes her wonder, once more, who this man she has fallen for really is.

His jaw works and then, in a split second, his lips are on hers, taking hers, punishing her with his kiss, punishing her with his desire.

His erection presses against her stomach. Outside the office door, activity hums, the office like a beehive, the constant comings and goings, the chatter, the noise. Natasha pulls back, trying to break away, but Adam only tightens his hold on her as his tongue massages hers, a slow sensual punishment that makes her knees weak.

Arousal flushes her skin, making her nipples hard and her breath short.

Finally, just as Natasha is beginning to relax into him, Adam breaks away, staring down at her, his eyes glistening with fury, his arm still around her waist, stopping her from backing away.

"How the fuck could you just leave?"

"I'm sorry." Her apology sticks in her throat. "I –"

"Not good enough." He interrupts her, tightening his grip on her, making her acutely aware of their difference in size and stature. "I told you I loved you. The least you could have done was tell me you were going back to him."

Natasha reels. His words are designed to hurt and he has succeeded beautifully.

"Going back to him implies I left him to begin with."

She tenses, afraid of how he'll respond, afraid of his anger. When he releases her, she stumbles back.

But Adam isn't done. He comes towards her, his hands balled at his sides as if he's barely able to keep a grasp on his rage, and he lowers his face so they are staring eye to eye. "What are you so afraid of?" he pushes, pursuing her as she backs away until her ass meets the desk.

He presses his palms flat into the desk on either side of her, towering over her, trapping her with his body. "Are you afraid of the way I make you feel?"

Desire courses through her and she hates the way she responds to him, the way just being in the same room with him makes her feel reckless.

"Are you afraid of surrendering? Of giving in to all the things you write about so eloquently?" His hot breath fans her face as he pushes her, never giving her a chance to respond. "Are you afraid that if you let go with me, you'll never recover?"

Anger and desire war within her as she pushes off the desk, getting her face close to his.

"Of course I'm afraid," she answers, breathing hard. "I'd be crazy not to be afraid." Rising up to her tip toes so they are standing nearly eye to eye, she continues, her emotions flying, wild, free, uninhibited as they usually are. "You terrify me. Saturday night was amazing. And frightening. If you only wanted my body, I'd give it to you in a heartbeat. That's how much you make me feel. But that's not what you're asking, is it?"

His arm darts around her, lifting her easily and depositing her on the desk, his lips finding hers and Natasha, overcome by lust, twines her fingers in his thick, black hair, pulling him closer. Her nipples, hard as rocks, chafe against the material of her blouse, making her wish that she were naked. His tongue dances with hers, igniting every inch of her, the kiss so potent she feels it between her legs. She spreads her legs and Adam presses closer, his erection hard and heavy even through his jeans.

And just as suddenly, he breaks away, stepping back to run his hand through his hair, his eyes flashing wildly. "I could tell Christopher," he says, licking his lower lip. "I could tell him everything. About Layla. About the club. What do you think would happen if he found out? Would he still love you unconditionally?"

Natasha stiffens as life imitates art and she can't remember if she wrote this scene or if she merely imagined it. "You wouldn't."

"Wouldn't I? I lied. When I told you one night would be enough, that if you told me to leave you alone, I would – I was lying. Now that I've tasted you, I'm not going anywhere."

"Adam…"

He shakes his head. "Natasha, you're in my veins and there isn't a chance in hell I'm giving you up. You consume my thoughts. I get that you don't want to hurt him. But let me tell you something. You aren't doing him any favors staying out of loyalty instead of love. That isn't kindness, that's pity."

"Fuck you." She spits the words in his face, sitting up straight.

He shakes his head, making a lock of hair fall in front of his left eye. "You'd be an idiot to walk away from this."

She shivers, hugging her arms around her waist and looking around the room, as if only now realizing where they are. Her office on campus.

Natasha swallows hard.

"I'll see you tonight," Adam says, leaving her sitting on her desk, panting, nipples hard, lips bruised, sex wet and impatient.

She drops her head to her hands, only now remembering that tonight is the prospective students reading and that her attendance, as a member of the MFA faculty, is required.

CHAPTER TWENTY-EIGHT

The Alumni Club, with its multi-tiered crystal chandeliers and curved staircases and picture windows overlooking Morningside Park, now bathed in evening shadows, always takes her breath away. Natasha turns from the window, taking in the room steadily filling with current and prospective students.

Sipping her wine, she wonders what she's doing here. How she got to this place. She knows, of course, that she will have to smile politely and tell each and every one of the new students who approaches her that the program is wonderful, lauding it, selling them on it, when she isn't so certain that MFA programs are worth it.

Instead, she wants to tell them to think long and hard before committing. That reading and writing is enough. Why spend the hundred grand just for a piece of paper, that ultimately, is meaningless.

Christopher, across the room, is discussing something with one of the other poetry faculty members and he lifts his head, his eyes finding hers across the room, and smiles.

She feels that smile like a kick in the stomach and she struggles to return it. In a few minutes, when everyone has had a chance to go to the bar for a drink, they will be asked to take their seats.

She spots Adam. He's impossible to miss, standing tall by the door, his eyes sweeping over the room and she knows that he's searching for her and that when he sees her, he will come for her.

She shivers, turning away.

She wants, more than anything, to be certain. Of anything. Instead, her life, which once seemed so simple, so definite, has been reduced to a series of questions without answers.

Her phone chirps and she takes it out, glancing at the screen, her heart pounding as she reads the message from Adam.

Seeing you now makes me want to drag you upstairs and fuck you, hard and fast.

Her fingers tremble as she shoves her phone to the bottom of her purse.

She gulps her wine, jumping in surprise when she feels a hand on her shoulder.

Adam, she thinks. But when she turns, Christopher is standing beside her, his hand on her shoulder.

"Hey." He bends down to press his lips to her cheek in a chaste kiss.

"Hey."

"There's someone I want you to meet."

"New student?"

He nods and Natasha drains her glass, setting it on one of the tables spread throughout the room. "Okay."

She follows him across the room to where a group of

prospective students gather around a small circular table.

"Carrie, this is Natasha Carson," he says to one of the women at the table, a girl, really, her face bright and innocent, the freckles on her nose and dusting her cheeks accentuated by the dark eyeliner around her big eyes.

The girl's eyes go wide for a moment and then she grins. "I loved *Hunger*," she says, surprising Natasha with her candor. Natasha, who has always considered earnest excitement to be the mark of a foolish person, doesn't know how to respond.

But the girl looks at her with such hope, something cracks inside of Natasha. She reaches out her hand, shaking the girl's hand.

"The pleasure is all mine," she says. When her phone chirps in her bag, she ignores it, focusing all her attention on the student in front of her. This, she reminds herself, is her job. As a mentor. As an example. Still, she finds it disgusting, conning these young people into turning over more money than they can ever dream of making as writers for the chance at what? Prestige? A degree they can hang on a wall somewhere, a black stain, a reminder of the dreams they once had?

The opportunity to be like her?

"Are you applying anywhere else?" she inquires politely.

The girl shakes her head. "No. This is where I want to be. I've known that for forever. I don't just want an MFA. I want *this* MFA." The girl grins foolishly, her assuredness surprising.

"What do you plan on studying?"

"Fiction."

"Well, we'd be happy to have you."

Over the loud speaker comes a voice, telling everyone to take their seats, that the discussion will be beginning shortly. Natasha reaches out her hand, once more shaking the girl's hand. "Good luck with the application process," she says before she and Christopher slip away, melting into the crowd of people angling for seats.

In the front row, little place cards mark out the seats reserved for faculty members and they remove them, sitting, waiting.

Natasha's phone chirps again and she glances at it quickly, seeing the messages from Adam that light up the screen.

He doesn't know you.

I want you.

I need you.

Talk to me.

She turns her phone off and focuses her eyes on the podium, willing the lights to dim, willing the event to begin.

"I never set out to be a humor writer. All through school I thought, I'll write the next very serious, very important novel. It will be important with a capital I. And all the while, as I was writing, I was miserable. My wife kept asking how it was going and I'd lie and say it was going great, that I was onto something, but we both knew the bottles were piling up in the recycling bin and I wasn't happy.

"We were having money problems and finally decided to sublet our place and stay at her parents' house, out in the country. Here I am, the ultimate New York City boy stuck on a farm in the middle of nowhere, the closest town

is twenty miles away and the grocery store closed at 5 pm
and nothing was open on Sundays and I thought, Oh god,
I am going to die.

"The truth was, my book was killing me and my wife,
bless her glorious soul, seemed to realize that long, long
before I ever did. And finally, she told me she was going to
leave me if I didn't put it aside and work on something else
for a while.

"Now, as I'm sure all of you know, as a writer, having
to choose between your baby and the person in your life,
it's not an easy choice. I had to think about it, and again,
my wife is a truly amazing woman, she didn't walk out on
me the moment I hesitated, and I'm not so sure I can say I
would have been quite so understanding if the tables had
been turned, but luckily they weren't, and eventually, I
agreed. I'd put it aside and focused on something else.

"It turned out to be the best thing that ever happened
for me, both personally and professionally. That
monstrosity of a book is still sitting, locked in the bottom
drawer of the file cabinet in my office and sometimes,
when I'm feeling a little low, I'll pull it out, just a big,
messy ol' stack of typewritten pages, and look at it, letting
it serve as a reminder that sometimes, the things you think
you should be doing, the things you think are important,
are in fact totally off-base. I have my wife to thank for
that. Wonderful woman. Really, just a fabulous woman."

Natasha's mind wanders as she only half listens to the
speaker. Somewhere behind her, in the crowd of students,
Adam sits, and she has little doubt that he's watching her,
making her strangely self-conscious anytime Christopher
leans in to whisper something in her ear.

She's torn. Between what she knows, at least on paper,

is perfect. And what she fears may be a mistake, but one she wants, desperately to make.

Whatever she does, she can't leave Christopher for Adam. Trading one for the other will change nothing. Will solve nothing.

Whatever she decides, it has to be her decision, one she makes for herself. And Natasha, staring at her hands, wonders when the last time was that she allowed herself to make a decision so selfishly.

On the walk home, neither speak. Their breath makes small puffs in the cool, fall air and halos ring the street lamps. Natasha buries her hands deep in the pockets of her jacket, her head tucked down, her scarf wrapped tightly around her neck.

With every step she takes, she knows the decision has been made and it is only a matter of acting.

The feeling only grows as they approach the apartment.

Once upstairs, Christopher sets the kettle on and unwraps two mint tea bags, putting them in mugs on the counter, never asking if Natasha would like tea.

Every action, every gesture, every little thing that once seemed so comforting, now takes on a stultifying air and Natasha feels like there is a great weight on her chest, making it impossible to breathe.

Tea made and cooling on the counter, Christopher begins to undress, loosening his tie and Natasha, unable to keep it in any longer, says, "Christopher, we need to talk."

He looks up, and she sees the moment when he realizes exactly what is about to happen, what she is about to say without her having to say it.

The pain in his eyes makes her stomach turn.

"Natasha, no." He comes for her, his eyes pleading and she forces herself not to look away. Not to shield herself from this.

Forces herself to stand up straight when what she wants is to run away and hide.

"I'm so sorry."

"Why?" he demands.

"I'm not happy," she admits, watching his face fall and his shoulders sag.

"We don't have to get married," he says hastily. "If you don't want to get married, that's okay. I just want to be with you. I love you. That's all that matters."

She swallows the lump in her throat, knowing what she must do. That she must hurt him. That she has already hurt him.

"But that's not okay," she says firmly. "You *want* to get married. You *want* kids and I can't do that. Not now. I'm not ready. And truthfully, I don't know if I'll ever be ready."

"I don't care about any of that. All I care about is you." The emotion behind those words takes her breath away and she almost caves, almost goes to him, letting him wrap his strong and familiar arms around her body, arms that have been her home for four years.

Instead, she stands just a little taller. "Christopher, you do care," she says, softly but with force. "I know you do. And I won't be the reason you give up on that. On kids. On having a family."

"Is there someone else?" His lips quiver and she worries, suddenly that he will begin to cry.

For a split second, she considers telling him the truth, but after all of the lies, this is not the moment. "No," she says, watching him sag with relief, "there's no one else."

"We can make this work. I can make this work. I can do more. Be better."

Her heart breaks apart, split into a million tiny shards by his insistence. She knows he loves her, knows that he would do anything to make her happy. But there's nothing he can do to fix this.

"Christopher."

"Do you love me?"

She blinks quickly, refusing to let him see her cry. "I will always love you," she says slowly. "But I'm not *in* love with you anymore."

She walks towards the closet and Christopher follows her. "What are you doing?"

She doesn't turn around, doesn't look at him because she knows what she will see in his eyes. The pain. The hurt. And the knowledge that she is both the cause and the only possible cure.

"I have to leave."

"Stay. Just for tonight. Please."

How tempting it is, just to give in, just to let him soothe her for one more night, but she can't give him that false hope. Now that her mind is made up, now that she has taken the first step, she knows that she must leave. Now. Before she can be convinced to remain.

"I can't."

"I love you."

"I know."

"Stay."

"No."

Hastily, she throws a few things into an overnight bag, while Christopher stands behind her, watching her. She doesn't need much, just enough to get her through the next few days. She can't think past that.

At some point, she'll have to come back for the rest of her things and the thought fills her with pain.

When she zips up the bag, Christopher walks her to the door in silence and then, when she thinks he can't do anything else to make her heart hurt worse, he says, "Do you have somewhere to go tonight? I just want to know that you're safe."

She looks into those beautiful blue eyes, fighting against the tears. She won't cry in front of him. She won't make him comfort her when she is the one to blame.

She rests her palm on his arm, squeezing gently. "I'll be fine, I promise."

With that, she walks out of the apartment that has been her home for three years, walks out on her life, and as the elevator slowly makes its way to the lobby, she begins to cry. The tears come hot and fast and she doesn't brush them away. She lets them fall.

The elevator doors open and she steps out into the night and for a moment, she just stares up at the sky, her tears glistening in the streetlamps.

She fills her lungs and slowly exhales.

She's free.

ABOUT THE AUTHOR

Katie Devoe grew up in New York City and has lived in Los Angeles, Madrid, and Barcelona. She's worked as a barista, bookseller, cheese-maker and organic farmer. Her idea of a dream day is curled up in a cozy sweater, drinking Fortnum & Mason tea, and reading.